The truth will set them free, or tear them apart.

SEQUEL TO
BEYOND THE HURT

More Than Enough

THE DEBRA TUCKER STORY

Akilah Trinay

Also by Akilah Trinay

Beyond the Hurt

SEQUEL TO
BEYOND THE HURT

More Than Enough

THE DEBRA TUCKER STORY

Akilah Trinay

This novel is entirely a work of fiction. The names, characters and incidents portrayed in it are the work of the author's imagination. Any resemblance to actual persons, living or dead, events or localities is entirely coincidental.

Copyright © 2025 by Sharifa Akilah Trinay Parr. All rights reserved. Printed in the United States of America. No part of this publication may be reproduced, stored or transmitted in any form or by any means, electronic, mechanical, photocopying, recording, scanning, or otherwise, without written permission from the publisher. It is illegal to copy this book, post it to a website, or distribute it by any other means without permission except in the case of brief quotations embodied in critical articles and reviews. For information, address Revision Publishing LLC, 4505 Montara Drive, Antioch, CA 94531.

Revision Publishing books may be purchased for educational, business, or sales promotional use. For information, please email contact@revisionpub.com.

First edition

Library of Congress Control Number: 2025907077

ISBN 979-8-9929944-1-4 (Hardcover)
ISBN 979-8-9929944-0-7 (Paperback)
ISBN 979-8-9929944-2-1 (ebook)

Developmental Editing by Nicole Walker
Cover art by Lucy Giller
Interior Design by Samia Asif

THE DEBRA TUCKER STORY

I dedicate this book to my loving husband, my beautiful daughter, and all my family and friends.

Dear Reader:

It has been a long time coming, but we are finally here. Please sit back and enjoy the ride you're about to embark on; journeying through the next phase of the story through the lens of Debra Tucker-Covington. She represents the relationship struggle between partners, self, and the world. You will find some explicit language throughout the story to maintain the integrity of the characters. Reader discretion is advised.

Prologue

Welcome back, here we meet again. Super dope that you all have stuck around to see about me. I'm grown now, like real-life grown. I've been through some trials, but I'm still here. A little broken, definitely bruised. And guess what? I still have a way to go.

Avoid healing, and you'll find yourself drawn to others who are broken, becoming entangled and trapped. While pain is fleeting, scars remain. The aim is to experience pain without letting it leave lasting marks. Scars lead to dwelling on past hurts, even though the pain itself is gone. But remember, a scar signifies healing. It's the lingering memories that haunt us. This understanding took me time to reach, time to become ready to share my story openly.

Our bodies have an incredible way of healing. When we're hurt, a scab forms, a testament to our body's attempt to regenerate. It's a process divinely designed for restoration. The way God created us, *He* intended for us to experience a healing process. Yet, we often interfere with this process, prolonging our pain by trying to be our own saviors, using ineffective strategies. I've realized I've delayed my own healing by constantly picking at my wounds, causing them to scab up, preventing true recovery. I've been on a journey of self-discovery, seeking solace in prayer and meditation to connect with my true self and the purpose I was created for.

Now, reflecting on my past, everything clicks. My actions, failures, and how I see the world all align. Oakland, a city of incredible beauty, is also a place of stark contradictions. A sharp contrast of wealth and poverty, downtown is undergoing a dramatic shift in atmosphere and culture due to the presence of multi-million-dollar companies and tech giants, and yet blocks away, Black men are still murdered in the streets.

When I was young, I was simply trying to navigate the world. My parents painted an overly optimistic, unrealistic picture of society, love, and family. They did what they could, but it wasn't enough. My mother, deeply wounded, clung to my father, willing to endure anything to keep him and the family together. She was chasing an idealized marriage, one that I suspect even she knew was a fantasy, but she was committed to making it a reality.

Edmund Tucker, *my daddy*, spent his days working and keeping the roof over our heads. He was important in the business world and brought that same energy home with him. He needed his wife to treat him like a king, his son to respect him at all times, and he just wanted me to be innocent. My daddy could not bear to learn, find out, or hear that his baby girl was whoring around the city. He had way too many eyes out in the streets for me to even consider that lifestyle.

The relationship between my father and Samson was always strained. Dad never felt a real bond with him and was convinced Samson didn't respect him. I saw it differently. Samson didn't seem interested in Dad's world or his money. He wanted a life on the streets, to earn respect there. It baffled me. Who would choose hardship when we had a good life? We had both parents, a nice house in East Oakland, freedom, and everything we needed. What else could we possibly desire?

I yearned for my mother's attention, even just half of what she gave Samson. I needed her guidance, for her to acknowledge the young woman I was. Perhaps, if she had, I wouldn't have been so easily swayed by my peers. I might have waited and not equated sex with adulthood. The lack of direction led to a pregnancy that I lost. I wanted her to be proud of me, but her focus was always on Samson, who never changed and continually caused problems. Living with them was challenging; she always shielded him, treating him like a child. He needed to be independent, but they fostered his dependence.

My father was the undisputed leader of our home, a ruler on his throne. He held power at his job and demanded absolute authority in our family life. Samson, driven by some inner need, persistently challenged this authority, as though trying to usurp the throne. These clashes were painful to watch, yet neither would yield. Finally, Samson seemed to grasp the situation and directed his energy elsewhere, finding his place among those who lived by the rules of the street.

The misconception is that we had more than enough. The reality is that we were trying to get beyond the hurt, to get to healing.

I am Debra Tucker. I am fractured; I am exhausted, and I am determined to heal and break free. This is *my* story.

CHAPTER 1

Week 1
Wednesday Early Evening

As I stepped into the building, my nerves flared, my hesitation intensified, but I knew this needed to be done to move forward. We are finally doing this. I could hardly believe we were finally here. We were doing the work, confronting our issues, taking life by the neck, and making this work! I felt a surge of pride, like giving myself a mental high-five. All my twenty-nine years, all the pain, had led me to this point. It felt right. Walking into the realm of release, to expose all our dirty laundry—ironically—felt right.

The office walls were primarily bare, except for this huge, framed picture, oddly positioned, right smack in the middle, of this generic-looking family, prancing in a meadow surrounded by ultra-white lilies. It was like stepping into some weird TV show, we were guest-starring in *The Twilight Zone*. Honestly, that picture felt like it was laughing at us, showing off this perfect life we could never have. A made-up world that I kinda wish I could just jump into and live in, for real.

Five o'clock on the dot. Strangely, we were on time, but in the business world, that's practically late. Usually, I ran on *his* schedule, *his* rules, but we were both itching to see if our family dysfunction really had a resolution. I was hanging by a thread. I think he was pretty much done with the whole thing.

Silence greeted us, heavy and still, it felt like we were the only people there. A chill hung in the air, a feeling like I was walking into something inevitable. I went up to the receptionist's desk. Derrick sank into a chair in the waiting area. It was our usual routine—leaving me to handle everything. The receptionist kept typing, not even bothering to glance at me. Her long, brightly painted nails clicked against the keyboard as I stood there, feeling totally ignored.

"Grab the clipboard, sign-in, and complete the paperwork. Fill in all the highlighted areas. The therapist will be with you shortly," she directed, batting her lashes at the computer screen, still not looking in my direction.

I sensed an attitude. *She really don't wanna mess with me today!* I expected exceptional customer care from the woman, considering the collective community plight; a look, a gesture, a *hey girl, wassup wit' you? What brings you in today?* Instead, I got nothing, but a stale face; and a stanky attitude for days. I wished she didn't, so we didn't have to play into the old-time stereotype of Black women not getting along. It was clear she forgot her loyalty amid all the "White" money that came flowing through the door. She probably thought we were broke. And who cares if she was right? It was not her place to judge. Although I make a decent living for myself, I was lucky to book this appointment. My boss had the plug and made a "special accommodation."

He hooked us up with four free sessions. I took a deep breath and shook off her energy. To keep the peace, I let her slide *this* time. I was not here for all that. Derrick and I had reached rock bottom and, between prayers and fistfights, needed as much intervention as possible.

"Here Babe, fill this out." I tossed the clipboard into his lap.

"I hope this doesn't take all day. You know I don't want to do this shit. I'm only here because I'm not ready to give up yet," he said under his breath, loud enough for me to hear, but low enough that no one else in earshot could.

Derrick kept reminding me it was my idea to go to therapy. As if I caused our relationship to go down in flames. As if it was my fault, he entertained ongoing relationships outside of our marriage. *I think not!*

"I still got love for you, D." He shot me a tender glance and pooched out his lips, his way of manipulating me into believing I was still the center of his world.

I readjusted in my seat and rolled my eyes. He was aware of his sexy lips, and he believed that whispering sweet nothings would make everyone forgive him. Yep, I was dickmatized. He practically isolated me from my family. He was in control of most things, including my peace, which was tied to my decision-making. If he said it, I was doing it. I kept my back towards him. I avoided making too much direct eye contact to not get caught in his trance. He was clever. Had me constantly reevaluating my actions to determine where things had gone wrong. *If he loved me, we wouldn't be in this mess. If he loved me, he would know how to keep his "peen" to himself and not flaunt it all over the Bay Area.*

"When we finish with therapy, things gotta change. I mean it!" I insisted.

"I'm doing *you* a favor by being here, sweetheart," he shot back, shifting uncomfortably and trying to stop his hands from moving so much. He'd actually resisted the urge to grab that last cold beer, making him even more irritable.

The therapist reiterated multiple times that to complete the therapy session meant to come sober. My husband took it to mean that getting hammered the night before is totally permissible. Naturally, he rolled in at three A.M., stumbling all over the place, waking me up out of my sleep for some late-night *nookie,* which I wasn't in the mood for. He got a few hours of sleep, technically going against her request. But, in his world, he was completely sober.

Then, just like that, my phone buzzed with a text. It was Mama:

> `Debra, just take it for what it is. Don't get too worked up.`

I told my mother we were trying therapy. I was going to take my own advice for once. She didn't know the details. Texting was her way of keeping things distant but supportive, playing it cool. She avoided asking too much about what was going wrong, not that she had much choice. My boundaries were rock solid, and she knew I'd just deny everything. Since I'd grown up, we'd gotten better at handling each other, we used some deescalating strategies I read about, like taking deep breaths and allowing wait time before proceeding with any tough conversations. But she wasn't really interested in the details of my life, since I married him despite her dissatisfaction. She blamed him for pulling me away and conveniently placed our mother-daughter bond on ice for a few months. Based on my mom's logic, his presence in my life was the cause of our issues. Trust, I didn't skip a beat, but this meant I had fewer outlets to process the breakdown of the relationship.

"Derrick, I'll be right back." I said. He nodded, picked up his cell phone, and started scrolling.

I exited the lobby and walked down the hall to the stairwell to get some fresh air. It was just my luck that the elevator was out of service. If I didn't respond quick enough, Mama would light up my phone with back-to-back messages being overly dramatic, in a panic, demanding a response. She was not tech-savvy, but she somehow conquered the text message function.

The moment I stepped outside into the city's crisp air, I was reminded of just how much I genuinely disliked San Francisco. As an Oakland native, I have always been loyal to my city. San Francisco was great for shopping and sightseeing, but the hassle of crossing the bridge, sitting in thirty to forty-five-minute traffic for what's normally a fifteen-minute ride, was utterly ridiculous. All the people, the congestion, and parking kept me far away. We took a ride-share service, omitting us from the obligation to pay the toll. Seven dollars to cross the bridge. Staying local was important, but finding a Black Therapist was the goal. Unfortunately for us, finding a Black therapist in Oakland who didn't know my family was nearly impossible. Bottom line, we couldn't find one, so we took a recommendation for Laura Schatz, a marriage and family therapist. I'm usually hesitant to trust White women, but after talking to her on the phone, I felt she could help us understand our dysfunctional lifestyle.

> Thanks, Mama. I'm alright. I'll come
> by this weekend to see you and Dad.

Message sent. *Please let that be enough.* I walked back inside, knowing it was time. I gave the universal one-minute signal, still huffing and puffing from the trek up the stairs. To my advantage, the cool air helped to chill my steadily increasing body temperature.

With a voice dripping with unnecessary attitude, she announced, "Alright, you two, grab your things and come on. And don't forget the highlighted parts of the paperwork." She attempted a smile, but it was about as genuine as a three-dollar bill, like she'd been drinking a 'tude smoothie all morning.

She reluctantly led us down a narrow hallway into a small, air-conditioned therapy room with two little beige couches that beckoned me to sink into. I scanned the room before making any movements. The set up was simple. A grandfather clock on the wall, a desk, and black chair. Off to the right of the couches was a small wooden table with ball-like decorations on display. The interior decoration was not my style, but I had to consider where we were. I noticed a bookshelf with marriage and communication books, probably just for show, or maybe the therapist really loved them. The room was tiny, but it had this peaceful vibe. I was feeling "fixed" already.

"Would you like water or something?" The receptionist muttered under her breath for formality. She turned and walked away, not waiting for a response, assuming that we would decline her offer.

"Strike two." I remarked in disgust. "She has one more time, babe, and I'm going to go straight *East Oakland* on her!"

"Sweetheart, please, you're more likely to go *Riverside* on her first." He joked, as if to strip me of my *Town Bizness* card.

"Hello and welcome." Mrs. Schatz said, entering with a pleasant smile. She was a middle-aged White woman, average build, with sandy brown hair piled into a messy bun. She wore a simple floral outfit that looked like she spent most of her days confined to her office. "I am delighted that you both could make it today. I understand this wasn't your first choice, but after speaking with Debra, I am confident this is the best decision for your relationship." She set down her worn notebook, sat, and set the timer on her phone to begin the session. She clasped her hands and took a deep breath. "Therapy is the best gift you can give yourself," she continued. "Whether you want to break a cycle, feel less hopeless, or connect with what truly matters, you made the right decision."

She kept making eye contact, like she was reading us. I sensed she was gathering information about our inner thoughts from our body movements. Black folks just have a different way of doing things sometimes. I wondered if she was a therapist, a mind reader, or something else entirely. Whatever it was, I was getting really uneasy. I snuck a peek at Derrick, and he was sitting upright, staring at her like he was totally confused, trying to decide if he really wanted to go through with this. He tried to slide his hand on my slightly exposed thigh, and I quickly pushed his hand away. She just watched with this little smile, like she was waiting for something.

She started off, sounding a bit like she was reading from a script. "My therapy is client-centered. We'll tackle your issues together, find your strengths, and come up with ways to cope. I hold a deep respect for those who try therapy." She paused and took in another deep breath. "Thank you for being brave, Derrick and Debra, for being open and wanting to make things better. We can make this a safe space to figure things out, understand each other, and heal." Then she closed her eyes. "Please close your eyes with me." It felt weird, but we did it. I suddenly felt like I could trust her. I listened first with my ears, then with my heart. Don't ask me how, but I was doing it. "Reflect upon a painful experience." Pausing again, she gave us a moment to center our thoughts. "Get in your mind." The room got super quiet. I could hear Derrick breathing loudly. It was all I could hear. I giggled a little; it was just so awkward. "Don't speak. Feel it." More silence. "Think about how it made you feel." She gave us another few seconds of meditation. "I wish to journey with you to that place. Take a deep breath." She paused again. "Now open your eyes. Mr. Covington, I shall start with you. Do you agree to go on this journey toward healing?"

Derrick looked totally confused. He cleared his throat and adjusted himself. I'd seen him nodding off during that little meditation. He cleared his throat again, like he was trying to wake himself up, and finally said, "I can't make any promises, but I'll try." He propped his right foot on his left knee and just held it there, like he was hoping that would be enough to satisfy me.

"I commend you for your courage to try," she continued serenely. "Many men are hesitant to participate in therapy, believing it's only for women or White people. As the head of the household, I applaud your willingness to step forward." He grinned, puffing out his chest a bit. I sighed deeply, remembering the weeks leading up to this moment, the arguments and fussing. It was all for show, but as long as he does his part, that's all that matters. She turned to me. "Debra, do you agree to take the journey toward healing?"

A moment passed, then I finally peered over at Derrick, took in another breath, and exhaled. I desperately wanted this to work, so I forced myself to soften up. I repeated his earlier gesture, running my hand over his thigh. "Babe," I said, "there's gonna be things that come up, things that are really hard for me to talk about. I need to know you'll be here, really here, through this entire process." He placed his hand on mine, and I gripped it tightly.

"I'm here, right? I got you!" with that classic *Smooth Operator* charm of his.

I returned my gaze to Mrs. Schatz. "Yes."

She nodded, acknowledging my answer. "Debra, as you were the one to make the initial call, I gather that you're the most invested party in this endeavor. Do you still consent to undertake this journey towards healing, even if your husband chooses to check out during the process? Before you respond, keep in mind, some of what we talk about won't be easy to hear."

"Yeah, I know all that, and yes, I agree," I blurted out. Honestly, her intro was taking forever.

"Okay, shall we dive in? We'll have ninety-minute sessions. Derrick, I was curious, on your form you listed 'children.' I understand Derrick Jr. isn't participating, as Debra mentioned, but I'm wondering about another child? Are you two expecting?"

"Wait, what?" I was totally lost. *Children?* I let that hang in the air for a second. "Expecting what? Another kid? What the hell?" I asked, knowing it was basically to myself. I knew about *my* pregnancy test, but he didn't. And honestly, I wasn't even sure what I wanted to do about it. It just didn't make sense. Why would he write "children" on the form? Was he digging through the trash? Or did he suddenly want to talk about having more kids? *Breathe, Debra.* This was why we were here. I looked at him, waiting for an answer. And waited. *Maybe he's messing with me? Yeah, it's a joke. Really funny.* I decided it was a joke and just said, "Derrick?" He just sat there, silent, in solidarity with his inner thoughts. *He wrote it on the paper. Why not talk now? Was I already regretting agreeing to this? Were there even more secrets I didn't know about?*

Apparently, I was the only one who had no clue. I was completely shocked and blindsided. The anger was just bubbling up inside me, getting stronger and stronger. I felt like I was about to explode. I looked him dead in the eye; I had no choice but to develop my own conclusions. Slowly, I felt moisture spread across my temple, and a sudden internal heatwave surged through me, sending my body temperature skyrocketing from a steady 98 degrees to a sweltering 105 degrees in a matter of seconds.

I was on my feet before I knew it, the words just exploding out of me. "Will somebody please tell me what's going on?"

Mrs. Schatz tried to get me to calm me down, but I wasn't having it. I'd suggested therapy to drag all the drama and secrets out into the open. I was done with his games. Staying with a man who couldn't fully commit, who couldn't give me his whole heart, felt utterly outrageous. I couldn't stand his silence for another second. I stared him down, my eyes searching his face for something, anything. But he still wore that same dazed, distant expression. I wasn't asking for the moon. It shouldn't take an eternity to give a simple answer. Yet, he continued to look at me like he was completely lost in space.

Derrick rubbed his forehead and dropped his head into his hands. "That night I told you about Tatiana," he mumbled. "I didn't know she was pregnant yet." He trailed off, saying something else I couldn't quite catch. *Was he talking to me, or just praying to God for help? Because he was definitely going to need it.*

"What?" I was trying my best to restrain. "Derrick, what the fuck are you saying?" I was practically breathing down his neck, and every nerve in my body was on fire.

Honestly, I didn't think I could still feel this way about him. Hearing him admit to cheating, even again, it hit me way harder than I expected. It had stung the first time, but this time, knowing he'd gone so far as to get someone pregnant, it cut much deeper. What was I even trying to save? Right there, right then, Derrick Paul Covington transformed right in front of my eyes. The man I held in high esteem. The man I fell instantly in love with years ago, who could say jump and I would respond with how high? Something shattered inside me. I didn't want to be connected anymore.

"Debra, please, try to remain calm. Perhaps you could take a seat on the couch, so we can sort this out," Mrs. Schatz requested, sounding a touch flustered. "Let us refrain from drawing conclusions until we have all the facts."

"I would love to stay calm, but I just heard all the facts. My *wonderful* husband hadn't said a single word about any of this. I really thought he was finally gonna be the man he promised, that we were gonna have a fresh start, but he'd been off playing house somewhere else, making a whole other family. Not knowing he had made a baby in two places. With his trifling ass!"

"Debra, what the fuck you mean, a baby in two places? You're pregnant?" Derrick questioned, with that fire in his eyes, looking like he was ready to pounce on me if I didn't answer him.

"I'd appreciate it if you would both avoid using profanity in this room," Mrs. Schatz requested, firmly reasserting her authority.

"Why does it matter?" I retorted. "So, we can keep up this bullshit fairy tale charade? So you can continue to play the poor, misunderstood victim?" I insisted, completely ignoring the therapist's request. *I was done with playing nice.*

Derrick jumped up, inches from my face. I knew if I uttered

another syllable, we'd be in a full-blown *Jerry Springer* brawl, the kind where you need Steve Wilkos to separate you. Yes, we got down like that. I clamped down on my lip to stop myself from saying something I'd regret and chose to retreat. All I wanted was to break down, but I wasn't about to show him any weakness. I remained silent. "Debra, you dragged me here. To fix our marriage, right?" I offered no response. Derrick's energy seemed to dissipate. He retreated slowly and sank back into his seat, mute. I watched as my words visibly took root in his mind. It was apparent we were a far greater challenge than Mrs. Schatz had anticipated. And a nagging doubt crept in: was she even equipped to deal with what we brought to the table?

Immediately, like she could hear what I was thinking, she jumped in, "I've been doing this for over ten years! Trust me, I've seen it all. And you might be surprised, but drama, trauma, and dysfunction aren't a *Black thing.*" She paused to get herself together, then added, "If you let me, I can help you through this!" She was trying hard to stay calm and in control. "Debra, please, sit back down so we can resolve this." She gestured, pointing to the empty seat beside my husband.

Almost like a domino effect, gravity pulled me back down to the couch. I allowed the pillows to absorb a portion of my frustration.

Mrs. Schatz shifted her attention entirely to Derrick, fixing on him with an almost hypnotic intensity. "Derrick, tell me about Tatiana. Talk to me directly. Debra, I just want you to listen." I didn't know if I wanted his story, but it wasn't my choice. Without hesitation, Mrs. Schatz pressed, "Who exactly is Tatiana?"

"Well... Mrs. Schatz." Derrick started, slowly creeping into his explanation.

"Call me Laura," she corrected.

"Uh, okay, Laura," he started, "before my son, even before I met Debra, there was this woman... Shayla. She had my heart. I was serious about her. I never told her, but I wanted to marry her."

The atmosphere in the room turned heavy. I felt a growing unease with his explanation, as if this was brand new information to me. I bit down hard on my lip, fidgeting with my hands, inspecting my cuticles with intense focus to avoid interrupting or letting my true emotions break through. Laura just listened intently, her blank facial expressions concealing her thoughts.

"We had a scare once before, when we were first dating," he explained.

"What are you talking about?, she asked about Tatiana." I interrupted, hoping to either get to the point or cease his confession.

He just kept going, like I hadn't even spoken. "She didn't know she was pregnant. We had a fight, nothing crazy, but she was stressed and had a miscarriage not long after. I was there for her for weeks, telling her I'd never leave. I felt so guilty, like my anger caused her to lose the baby. But I swear, I never touched her. It just got really hard to be around her. She was so moody, and it was too much. I just wanted to be happy." His eyes wandered up the wall, like he was looking at something way off in the distance, somewhere I'd never seen him go before. They were kinda watery, and he reached for my hand again, but I was frozen. He ended up just putting his hand on my wrist, gently holding it. "Debra knows," he said, "all I've ever wanted was a family. I didn't have that growing up, and I wanted it so bad!"

"You know I'm unable to have children! Please, don't do this to me. Not again!" I cried out with raw emotion. Tears threatened to spill over, and I desperately tried to stop the single tear from escaping my left eye, down my cheek, staining my crisp white blouse. This wasn't a fresh wound, but the pain was as raw and profound as ever.

"You know the story, a young Black male growing up in a single-parent household in the hood. Blah, blah, blah. Father wanting to live the single life, not wanting anything to do with our family." He looked over at Laura for acknowledgement. "I intended to be different, to break the cycle. Or at least that is what I wanted to do. I didn't want to be a statistic, but I ended up being just like that man in more ways than one. To be quite honest, I loved that girl! She was my first love and that ain't something you just get over."

"Debra, how does it make you feel to hear him speak about this woman, Shayla, in this way?" Laura questioned.

I hesitated, then admitted, "I've always known how much he wants a family, and it really hurts. It breaks my heart that someone else has this... hold over me. I might have the ring, but it feels like she has his heart. She and all the others, they always have." *It was the truth, and it stung.* Laura nodded, acknowledging my words, and then turned her attention back to Derrick.

"Shayla and I had an on-again, off-again thing going for years. She was seeing another cat, but I didn't sweat him. No other man ever intimidated me. I knew what I had with her, I knew how I made her feel. How else would I have been able to keep her coming back?" he asked, like it was obvious. "Then she shows up, says she's pregnant. Initially, she tried to deny it was mine, but eventually, after three long years, she admitted the truth. At first, I wanted no part of it, but I'd always wanted a son. So, I stepped up. He was my flesh and blood, and she named him Derrick. I knew what it felt like to be rejected, and I couldn't do that to my own child."

"You say it like it was not a big deal, but what were you truly feeling at the time?" Laura pulled for more.

"I was becoming a *simp*. I was spending less time with my boys, and I got caught up. She had my nose wide open. I was 21. A little *nigga* that thought he could do it all, that he could handle whatever the world threw his way. To be honest, I was terrified. I wanted out. I felt trapped, like I couldn't breathe. It was tough. I started working more, throwing money at the situation, trying to be the man I thought I should be. But I was resentful, and I treated her differently. Every time I tried to help, I just ended up pushing her further away. Eventually, we both called it quits. She moved on. I broke my promise to her, just like my dad did to my mom, so I felt like I had to be there for her whenever she needed me. I owed her that much." Derrick took a deep breath.

"To clarify, what do you mean when you say 'whenever she

needed me'?" Laura questioned.

"Whoever I was with, if she called, I went. I'd do anything. Like taking DJ–Derrick Jr.–and spending family time. Debra knew about her when we were dating," he added, trying to make it sound like it wasn't a secret.

Laura turned to me, looking really puzzled. "Debra, is this accurate? You knew about Shayla and you still stayed with Derrick?" she asked, even more confused now than before he started talking.

I snapped. "I was aware, but it is not what you think!" I felt a pang of embarrassment, acknowledging the judgment about my choice to remain with a man who'd been unfaithful.

Derrick tried to explain, "Debra only knew part of it. What man tells everything? I lied, kept secrets. Lied to keep her, said we weren't still seeing each other when we were."

Laura, still trying to figure out the whole "other children" thing, asked, "So, when does Tatiana come into all of this?"

"But Laura, I was doing everything to make Derrick happy, and he was just hurting me, hurting us!" I was more frustrated by the minute. "He only ever thought about himself," I said sadly. I couldn't help feeling sorry for myself, but also kinda guilty at the same time. It hit me, I'd married my dad, like I'd found a replica of him. Even though I'd judged her, I'd ended up in the exact same spot as my mother.

"Remember, there's no judgment here. I'm just trying to help you understand how you feel and why you make the choices you do, so you can heal. The more you talk about it, the better." Laura reminded, trying to get me to focus again.

"Thinking back, Derrick made me feel so special, like nobody else ever had. He had this way of making me feel like I was the only girl in the world," I said, remembering. "Back then, all I wanted was to be loved and accepted. And Derrick gave me that. He loved me, he knew everything about me, all my messed-up parts. He made me promise I wouldn't be like the others, like the man who meant the most to me–my dad." The tears started coming, and I couldn't hold them back. It hit me then, what my mama had told me in the hospital years ago. Seeing how she loved my dad, even after everything, made me think I could do the same with Derrick. She never gave up on him, and that was the example I followed.

I peered over at Derrick. His head in his hands. A broken man. How can two broken souls make it in love? I prayed hard to not be a part of the generational curse. It felt like *déjà vu*.

I vividly recalled the unfolding of the drama in my childhood; we sought counseling. The woman from the plane offered her services, and we all participated as a family. I'm still not sure if it was the right decision. I could hear the confession from my mother replaying in my head. *Well, he didn't act alone, having my suspicions, and I did my own investigating and found out what was going on. I did my dirt as well. I had my own affairs too!* My mother, Charlene Tucker, admitted to stepping out on my father. My jaw dropped, and my body clammed up. I could not take it anymore, and frankly, felt I didn't have to. As if the floor was exploding in that moment, the earth opened up right beneath me and the world as I knew it shattered and descended into the abyss. Immediately, I popped out of my seat and stormed out of the door, not prepared for the confession. I didn't have a clue, and no longer cared about the truth. All I needed was for the picture-perfect life my parents created to be my reality. I desired to be blind in order to avoid heartache and pain. That was the moment I became numb.

Laura cut into my thoughts, saying, "There is a significant amount of work ahead of us. This process will require time and cannot be resolved in a single session. We'll schedule our next session, but until then, I want you both to make a list. Write down five things you love about your partner, and next to each one, write down what you do to make that thing grow. Bring the list next time." She gave us a quick, reassuring smile. "I know we've opened up some old wounds today. Please be mindful that you're both feeling fragile, and avoid rehashing this conversation without me present. I understand it won't be easy, but trust the process, it really can help."

CHAPTER 2

Week 1
Friday Early Evening

Motionless, I sat on the train, my gaze fixed on the rhythmic passing of light posts outside the window, the images triggering a flood of memories leading to this moment. It was a haunting reflection of the turbulent shifts my life had undergone. I was constantly plunged into darkness, then momentarily emerging into light, as the train sped through tunnels. The events of the therapy session had only intensified my turmoil. I was torn, grappling with the agonizing question: *do I remain, or do I walk away? Could I truly accept the end of our covenant?* At each stop, the train car filled with more passengers, further overwhelming my already strained ability to process my thoughts.

The vibration from my phone, *Bzzz! Bzzz!,* jolted me, but my intention was to just ignore it and remain in my tranquil state of mind. *Bzzz! Bzzz!* He was persistent. It was like he knew I was trying to ignore him, so he was ready with a barrage of texts to blow up my phone. *Bzzz! Bzzz! Bzzz! Bzzz! He will not steal my joy today!* I told myself. But I had to get him to stop. I inhaled deeply and answered.

"What's for dinner, tonight?" he requested with no formal greeting or temperature check. Here I am, exhausted from counseling and supporting all the kiddos at work, and his only concern is himself.

"How about a proper greeting first before you come at me making requests?" I rebutted sarcastically.

"Ain't nobody got time for that! You're my wife, stop trippin.' Can you pick me up something on your way home? I'm in the mood for shrimp tacos or carne asada fries for dinner." He placed his order with me, as if I was taking his order at the drive-thru window.

Following the therapist's advice, I refrained from addressing that conversation during the first session. Honestly, I was afraid to touch it. Derrick wasn't great at talking things out, and we definitely weren't in a good spot to have a real conversation. Our disagreements could become very childlike, likened to playground put-downs, and not-so-loving "love taps." I felt like he probably "loved" me, but I wasn't sure if he even liked me. I was increasingly plagued by doubts about whether attempting to mend our fractured bond was a worthwhile endeavor. I knew about Tatiana, and yet, I stayed. I always stayed. In a weird way, it made things easier, because he wasn't around as much, and that was actually good sometimes. I kept hoping he'd just magically change, that I'd like him again, that we'd go back to how we were when we first met.

"So, yeah. Anything else you need?" I asked, trying to keep my voice even.

"Nah. That's it. I'll see you when you get here."

I ended the call and tried to reconnect with the tangled web of thoughts that had been occupying my mind.

A young couple, definitely in the middle of an argument, got on the train. The woman, average size, grabbed the center pole for balance. Her partner, about the same size, stood nearby, feet spread wide. We approached the next stop and a large man in construction clothes boarded, smiling at everyone. The train jolted, causing us all to lurch forward. The young lady against the pole stumbled and brushed up against the large man's back. They shared a laugh, and she apologized for the accidental touch. Her partner, however, was visibly displeased. He moved toward the construction worker. Another lurch, and the woman quickly positioned herself between the two, her hands on her boyfriend's face, a silent warning not to escalate. He shook her off, muttering something offensive, as if needing to assert his toughness.

Taking B.A.R.T. was always an unpredictable experience, a constant source of unexpected encounters. You'd see everyone, from high school kids blasting music to the random panhandlers and their young children, just trying to get a hotel room for the night. Yet, it is what I loved about the Bay Area. The sharp edges of danger softened by pockets of tranquility, the explosion of artistic expression against a backdrop of urban desolation. The ways that the young and old disregarded the rules, such as no loud music or panhandling, while being heavily policed. It was my home, a place of extraordinary diversity, steeped in history, and fueled by a long-standing commitment to political and social justice. Often, families had to adopt the grit necessary to survive in this place.

"Twelfth Street," the automated voice announced. I grabbed my stuff and jumped off before the doors slammed shut. The platform was packed, people going every which way. I dug in my pocket for my Clipper card to get out of the station. As soon as I cleared the barrier, I heard my name faintly called off in the distance. Debra's pretty common, so I tried to ignore it and keep moving, I was already late. Growing up in Oakland, you learn not to answer to just anyone. You never know who's looking for trouble. I remembered this story Big Mama used to tell us, about minding your own business. She said this woman heard her name called, turned around, and got killed. I don't even know if it was true, but Big Mama always told us these stories to scare us straight. Still, her stories stayed in my mind, and I used them as a form of precaution.

"Debra... D, hold up... Debra Tucker!"

My entire government, though. I turned slowly to acknowledge the voice, as now it was clear they were trying to gain *my* attention.

"Damn, Debra. You didn't hear me calling you?"

"Jamel! Oh my God! How've you been? What are you doing here?" Shock barely covered it. I was frozen for a moment, unsure whether to embrace him or offer a formal handshake. I had a million questions, but I held them back. I had to play it cool, hide how excited I really was. "I haven't seen or heard from you in what feels like a lifetime."

"You look good!" His eyes raked over me with a slow, deliberate appraisal. A knowing smile played on his lips, the kind that suggested he was confident he could still get it. "Real good," he repeated. "Hmm. You haven't changed at all. I spotted you right away and just had to come say hi." He looked me up and down again, rubbing his hands together.

Back in the day, Jamel was *that* dude. I mean, he was really *that nigga*. He had all the little girls on his jock; me included. He was Estelle's older cousin, my childhood crush, and, well, my first. Gone was the lanky boy of 5'11. He'd filled out, standing a good 6'2 and looking to be about 200 pounds. *Okay, Debra, focus*, I thought to myself, but the truth was, he could still get it!

"This is such a surprise. I didn't think I'd see you again. You look good." I suddenly felt like that awkward young girl I used to be. I glanced at him, my eyes landing on his wedding ring. "So, you're married now? Well, congratulations." I wasn't sure if I was actually happy about it, but I knew I had to acknowledge it.

"Thanks. Yeah, we've been married for three years. It's still kinda new, but it's good. I'm glad I finally settled down and found someone who's got my back." He paused and smiled, twisting his ring around his finger. "I don't see a ring on your finger. You mean to tell me yo' fine ass ain't settled down and had four babies by now?"

I paused, wrestling with whether to share the truth with this once-familiar stranger, or to keep it guarded, knowing that the truth often seemed to hold little weight. "Uh, I've been married for about five years," I said. "And things... aren't great. So, I'm not wearing my ring right now. Not until things get better." I held my breath, watching his face to gauge his response.

"So, he cheated?" he asked, looking a bit worried.

"Right now, things aren't great, so let's just leave it there," I said, cutting him off on purpose.

"Okay, sweetheart. I'll leave it alone, but if he ain't treating you right, you don't have to put up with that. I always tell my sisters, we men often don't realize what we have until it's gone, and then the next woman benefits. Don't let him practice being no good on you. I remember how you were back in the day, and I always knew you were different. You didn't run around like the other girls." He reached for my hand and stepped closer, like he was about to tell me something important. "When I thought about settling down, I wanted someone with your energy."

Here I stood, a grown woman, and yet I was still reduced to a giddy schoolgirl in his presence. He knew exactly what he was doing. I couldn't stop grinning like an idiot. Then, like a switch being flipped, everything stopped. I was transported back to the sterile hospital room, the rhythmic pulse of the machines echoing in my ears, the oppressive silence, the cold walls. He stood before me after all these years, unaware that we had once shared a secret, that we had created a child together. This man, who had seemed like the embodiment of my dreams, had gotten me pregnant without even knowing it. I'd lost touch with Estelle, so I didn't know how to reach him. It terrified me. And when the doctor told me I'd lost the baby, I buried everything deep down and left it all in that hospital room.

I squeezed his hand back. "That's really sweet of you to say. Too bad my husband doesn't see it that way," I said, looking away so he wouldn't see my eyes watering. "It's been so good seeing you. I really wish we could talk more, but I've gotta get to this appointment." I'd almost forgotten all about it, I was so caught up in the moment.

"Take my card. All my information is there." He finally released my hand. "Take care of yourself, sweetheart, and call me if you need anything."

And like that, we parted. I placed his card directly in my bag and moved swiftly to make up the minutes lost in conversation.

A cool evening breeze slipped through the security screen. It was still weird to me how dark it got by 4:30 P.M. Raquel Simmons kept the screen open to save on air conditioning and the energy bill. Despite her profits, she was meticulous about overhead, preferring to spend on herself. Business had been slow lately. Her original RQ Hair Care Salon, now a salon and barbershop run by Tanya, remained her biggest earner. Ironically, business had boomed after Calvin Rogers's murder, as people flocked to the area. She also benefited from Calvin's will; he'd promised to take care of her, and he did. She promoted Tanya and opened a downtown location for private appointments.

Moving back to Oakland didn't make me feel bad about still going to Raquel. Her beef with my mama wasn't my business. Our relationship was solid, all things considered. After all that drama, Raquel had decided she wasn't going to just sit around and be sad. She was gonna get back to work and make some money. Besides, she was still the best stylist around. Yeah, she was slow, and some of her styles were a little old-school, but nobody could do edges like Ms. Simmons. She was worth every second and every dollar.

"Hey, Miss Thang! Have a seat. Just finishing up with Lanette here," she called out as I came in. "You look tired. Grab something to drink if you want; you know where it is." She gestured vaguely while still concentrating on what she was doing.

"Yeah, I'm a bit tired. I rushed to get here on time, you know? Hi, Lanette," I said, sarcastically now that I realized I could've slowed down and engaged with Jamel longer. His attention had been surprisingly refreshing.

"It'll be five minutes."

I couldn't help but roll my eyes. *On time? What stylist is ever on time?* I've been getting my hair done for years, and it's never happened. And of course, the second I finally got comfy on the couch, I suddenly had to pee.

"I gotta run to the bathroom real quick," I said, basically telling her it was okay to take a bit longer as I maneuvered to the back of the salon. Raquel knew how to create a vibe. Her space was a feast for the senses, with studio lighting, music filling the air, striking Black art adorning the walls, area rugs adding warmth, vibrant colors popping everywhere, and, of course, the refreshments! You could choose anything from water to coffee to tea, hot chocolate, and even wine, depending on your mood.

"Girl, I am so glad that the shop is back open; my edges could not take another month without your magical hands," Lanette proclaimed, climbing out of Raquel's chair, checking herself out in the mirror. She smoothed down the few wild hairs on her forehead.

"I know that's right!" I joined in to affirm my intent to get into her chair as quickly as possible.

She laughed, "Girl, hush up!" She gestured for me to come to her station. Raquel noticed my new-growth and continued, "You can't rush perfection, but I can see you're in desperate need." She patted my shoulder and shook out the black cutting cloth, placing it around my body and returned her attention to Lanette. "Honestly, after everything with the investigation and getting this place cleaned up, I wondered if I'd ever reopen. Thankfully, I'm not a one-trick pony!" She nudged Lanette again, letting her know she wasn't about to let anything stop her hustle. Raquel then carefully guided my head down to begin trimming my edges before applying the relaxer to the back.

"Rocky, please forgive me for being rude. I'm truly sorry for everything you went through." Lanette said, grabbing her hand for emotional support. "I know that you and Calvin had your fair share of issues, but I know you still loved him." She'd been Raquel's friend and client for years, and she'd seen Charles grow up through all the ups and downs, along with his struggle toward reaching adulthood. "I know it's been a while since he died, but with that whole trial and everything, having to go through all that again... it must have been so much to handle."

"Hell yeah, it was tough. I closed my shop in Piedmont for a good two years before I could even imagine going back there."

I remained silent. It was my right. I just soaked it all up, letting the elders enlighten me on what the streets have been saying.

"I get it." Lanette paused and let her words linger for a moment.

"You know, Nette, honestly, it hasn't been as awful as I expected. I've had a lot of time to think and heal, and what's really getting to me is that I haven't talked to Charles. I still have days where I just cry, but I go for a run and it helps me clear my head. But it doesn't change the fact that my boy is still mad at me, and it's killing me. The last time I saw him, at Elijah's funeral, he just shook his head like he was disgusted. Wouldn't even talk to me about it." She quickly dabbed at her eye before a tear could fall.

"I'm sure he'll come around. You just gotta give him time."

"Twelve years ain't time?"

Lanette shot back, "You dropped a bomb on that young man. Imagine if you found out who your actual father was by accident?" I stayed perfectly still, staring at the floor. Raquel was good, but I wasn't taking any chances with her scissors. I didn't want any extra length coming off the back of my scalp.

"Girl, remember I was there." Raquel countered. "You know, I wanted to tell him as soon as he was old enough to get it, but the time was never right. And then, when Calvin became his enemy, I knew I couldn't tell him something like that. Charles, if given the chance, would have pulled that trigger."

"Look, no excuses. I'm your friend, so I gotta keep it real. You had ample opportunity to tell him years ago, but you chose not to. You wanted Edmond to leave that woman and live happily ever-after with you and Charles." Lanette spoke plainly, not mincing words. "Oh? You have nothing to say?"

I had zoned out of the conversation, but attention snapped back when I heard my father's name.

Raquel paused for a second, then finally broke her silence, "You're absolutely right," she confessed. "And Debra is fully aware of it. I was in love with her father, and I wanted him to leave Charlene. I truly did. But this is something I would never admit to anyone else."

The audacity of this woman to not flinch about the subject in my presence oddly made me feel more comfortable. The thing that made me respect Raquel was her honesty. My mother spent years in denial lying to herself, to me, her husband, and Samson. Raquel kept it real, and I admired her for it.

"You ain't gotta tell me! I *know* you!" Lanette was intimately familiar with the situation. She had spent countless hours, year after year, in her styling chair, listening to the unfolding drama of the Edmond and Charlene saga.

"That's easier said than done. And since you like to turn things around, imagine if the real father didn't want anything to do with the child? Then what?" Raquel questioned.

"Been there, done that, along with the hundreds of other women who have experienced the same thing. Truth is, as women, we can't allow men to get off so easily."

Raquel quickly interrupted. "Well... they *ALL* weren't dealing with Calvin Rogers."

"Girl, get out of yo' head. Calvin fathered plenty of children and left many mothers to figure it out on their own." Lanette hesitated a moment and noticed me still in the chair. "I gotta get going, but walk me to my car really quick, so I can give you your tip."

Raquel understood the code, as did I, and followed her out of the salon to have the rest of the conversation in private. Even though I could still hear everything.

"Look, you know what they're saying at the precinct, right? That Samson, Edmond's son, is actually Calvin's son, and he's getting out soon." Lanette paused to let that sink in. "So, Charlene was involved with both of them? And you have Debra sitting in your chair? What on earth is going on with you?"

"Trust me when I say I wasn't worried about that woman then and sure as hell ain't worried about her now." She rolled her eyes dramatically. "I make it my business to know everything." Raquel knew everything, obviously. Her clients were everywhere and many of the officers she met told her anything and everything she wanted to know. It was only fitting that she had the inside scoop.

"Why wouldn't she?" Lanette retorted. "Because he was with *you*? Charlene's gorgeous. She could snatch your man in a heartbeat! Plus, she let Ed play both sides, back and forth to your bed." Lanette Banks, a forthright woman of fifty-three, contentedly divorced and beaming with pride over her twin sons' college achievements, never hesitated to speak her truth.

"See? That's your thing, always looking at what everyone else is doing. I'm an adult. Calvin lived fast and liked women who were different."

"Okay, Rocky. I'm just trying to help and look out for you."

"Thanks, but I'm good. You got me out here thinking there was a tip," Raquel said, holding out her hand for the money so she could get back to her client.

"That *was* your tip!"

Rocky turned, gave her the finger, and walked away.

"See you in two weeks!" Lanette called out, smirking to herself.

"Yeah-yeah, I'll see yo' ass in two weeks."

When the salon door opened, it pleased me I would finally get to have my edges laid. All week, I'd been patting my head super gently to avoid scratching. The last thing I needed was for my scalp to burn. She prepared the relaxer mixture and applied the protective gel to my edges. As Raquel began the relaxer application, I couldn't stay quiet anymore. She seemed so lost in her conversation with Lanette, like she forgot I was even there. It was getting awkward, and honestly, I was curious about what they were talking about.

"You know, we never really found out for sure if Calvin was actually my brother's dad," I said, trying to fill the quiet.

"Debra, you and I both know that Calvin Rogers is Samson's father. Those years of the so-called love triangle? Charlene was no fool, and certainly no angel. We all managed because we all had secrets we kept. In my opinion, anyone past thirty has skeletons in their closet they're taking to the grave. If they don't, they haven't truly lived." Raquel stated matter-of-factually.

"I get it." My whole life has been about secrets. I literally just bumped into the guy who got me pregnant, and I just stood there, didn't say a thing. "For so long, I judged my parents so harshly for how they lived. I didn't understand any of it. To me, life was simple, and decisions were easy to make. Then I got a taste of life and realized that I was being corrupted and my perspective started changing."

"Oh, it happens to the best of us. For me, it started really young." She remarked with a casual tone. Raquel parted my hair and applied the relaxer to the roots. "You know, I met your father in high school. We started dating when I was sixteen. And here's the thing, he wasn't my first, not by a long shot." I shut my eyes as she brushed the cool chemicals throughout the parts of my hair. It was easier to just listen. Raquel wasn't embarrassed about anything in her life. That chair wasn't just for us clients, it was like therapy for her, too. And she kept talking. "Edmond was a good man, I knew it. He wasn't like all those other guys who were always coming on to me. He was sweet, kind, and really special." I could practically hear her smile as she thought about my dad. It was strikingly similar to how my mother had always spoken of him. It even crossed my mind that he might have been doing some sort of voodoo on these women, since his family *was* from New Orleans. "Ed was different from what I was used to." She paused for a second. "Look, I didn't have the 'perfect' life, but it wasn't bad. People always think if you don't have two parents, your life will be terrible." She shook her head hard. "Nah, I don't believe that. My life was just... different."

"Yeah, I know exactly what you mean," I added, wanting to contribute to the conversation. "My students come from all over Oakland, and seeing their different lives every day, it really shows you how different everyone's situation is."

"Exactly," she said, then jumped right back to what she was saying. "I wasn't afraid of my sexuality or my body, but I was aware. I developed early and understood what that meant. At nine years old, men started looking at me... differently. That's when I *knew*."

She seemed like she was about to tell me something really personal about when she was nine, but I didn't want to push it. So, I just changed the subject to steer the conversation in a different direction.

"How did you meet Calvin?" I questioned.

"It's strange, I can't remember when I first met Calvin, he was just always there. But I do remember... We were intimate for the first time when I was just fourteen."

"Are you serious?" I blurted out, turning so fast she nearly dropped the brush. I tried to just listen, but I couldn't.

"Girl, keep your head still or I'm gonna get this relaxer in your eyes." She gently guided my head back into place with her hands. "Calvin was my first, let's make that clear. He taught me the game, every bit of it. What men want and how they want it."

"Calvin taught you how to sleep around?" Now *I* was getting bold.

"He taught me how to survive in a world that wants to chew you up and spit you out. I learned how to protect myself and get money."

My curiosity was at its peak. I really wanted to know everything. I wanted her to tell me the code, the playbook, the game, but I was too scared to ask.

"With your dad, it was different. He saw who I really was, my heart, what I wanted to do with my life. He wanted me for more than my body."

It was like everything just fell into place, like the stars lining up, and things finally made sense. I felt a deep sense of relief to know my dad wasn't some heartless man who wanted to break my mother's heart. Similarly, my mother wasn't a naïve woman who had been controlled by his iron fist. She possessed her own hidden truths and would exert every ounce of her influence to prevent my father from leaving. She wasn't any different from Raquel.

As she finished up with my hair, she really opened up. Told me everything—the good, the bad, the whole story about my dad and Calvin. My phone chimed with a notification, and I glanced down to see it was Derrick. A faint hope flickered within me that perhaps there was an unexplored dimension to his character, something that might make me feel some compassion.

What time will you be home? I'm hungry!

I ignored it. I knew there'd be a fight later about me not replying, but I didn't care. Getting him his food was as much as he was getting from me tonight; end of story!

CHAPTER 3

Week 1
Saturday Afternoon

The excruciatingly long work week along with the changes to my body due to the pregnancy had me exhausted. My mission: to get out on a beautiful Saturday afternoon; just what the doctor ordered. Of course, not the actual doctor, because my appointment was not set for a few more days. I pulled up to my parent's house, filled with an array of emotions, resulting in a roller coaster of fatigue mixed with anxiety. I parked in my usual spot, right in front of the house, in between the neighbor's broken-down Buick and the start of our driveway, where I knew Daddy could see me. *Breathe. Inhale. Exhale.*

The most recent three-hour-long blow-up between me and Derrick had me on edge. I came home later than he desired with cold shrimp tacos from The Fish Grill. The truth is, I ignored his barrage of annoying text messages and non-stop calls. If I was a drinker, a Hennessy shot would have been my nightcap beverage, but unfortunately, the circumstance growing inside of me did not allow that option. I needed some peace. The fussing and constant fighting had to have an expiration date. I desperately needed a moment to come up for air. We only had one therapy session in the books and did our best to trust the process.

Derrick was stressing me out way too much, and it wasn't good for me or the baby. Mama had been on my case about not visiting, so I finally went over. It was long overdue. I figured I could get lost in their drama and forget about mine for a bit. I'd been avoiding them for weeks to dodge talking about my relationship problems. Honestly, all Mama could think about was Samson getting out of prison soon. My stuff just didn't seem to matter to her.

Charlene Tucker's beloved Samson. My big, knuckleheaded, misguided, and overly coddled brother was about to be free. Twelve years he'd spent locked up. When Mama found out that Samson had actually been responsible for the murder, she went into a deep depression, blaming herself for her own choices. She had never fathomed him capable of such an atrocity. She fought tirelessly for his freedom, sacrificing everything they owned. She put a lien on the house to cover court appeals and legal fees. Among other things, within the last year, life dispensed everything in its arsenal to wipe her completely out. Then Big Mama died, which hit us both hard. I loved Big Mama. This meant, for every visit, I had to carry Mama's pain, knowing she wouldn't do the same for me.

Breathe.

I shut my eyes. I took a second to gather myself, to calm down. I felt all shaken up inside. My mind went back to my reasons for being there. I remembered the first day I got home from school...

***

The mail came exactly at three, like always. The mail carrier took out the letters Mama had written to Samson and put in his letters for us. Mama was always watching from the window. As soon as the mail was dropped, she'd rush out to grab it, like it couldn't wait another second. She was the only one who ever wrote back to him, for all of us.

I, personally, was not comfortable communicating with my brother in this fashion. In so many ways, I was still in disbelief that it was really happening. Even though he needed a mandatory time out, to sit down and reflect on his actions, he was not cut out for prison, just like he was not cut out for the street life. I was afraid that he would get mixed up with the Northern Mexicans in a dispute over a 3-inch toothbrush. Better yet, he would meet Aabid Abdullah, convert to the faith of Islam, and become a master of the Quran. He would become intellectually unreachable or, worse, not come out at all. Admittedly, I watched too much television. In my mind, he was experiencing everything I witnessed on *Lockup*. However, my mother could not let a letter go unanswered, especially since it was her firstborn. The jealousy mixed with resentment couldn't help but fuel my negativity. I thought back to the time, years ago, in the hospital, when I was unable to reach my mother; and she was damn near knocking down the mailman to see if her baby boy was alright. He is a full-grown man—*I* was the child. I don't mean to sound insensitive, but he brought it upon himself. It is not like he was unconscious of the outcome. Uncle Dom, Cousin Fat-Fat, Black Rob, who stayed down the street, and Big L were perfect examples of a life in the streets gone wrong.

All that family drama was crazy, so I ended up taking a year off from U.C. Riverside. I told each of my professors of the situation. Sarah allowed me to remain her roommate until things died down a bit, although she spent the majority of her nights with her boyfriend, Brad. Trying to study with Mama calling me all the time and having to drive back and forth from Riverside to Oakland was not exactly the college experience I was hoping for. Thankfully, the majority of my professors were accommodating and allowed me to complete alternative assignments, preventing me from losing all my academic credits.

As expected, Mama knocked on my bedroom door. "Debra? Honey, come to the living room, please! Your brother's letters have arrived," she announced.

Edmond Tucker was the complete opposite. He elected not to participate in story time. Ever since he found out in therapy that Samson wasn't his, he changed. Strangely, he never voiced it, at least not in my presence. I'm sure he felt it was his karma. When I walked out of that family therapy session, the therapist ended the session and gave us a date and time to return, paired with our homework assignment to write out all the burning questions we had for each other. She said that nothing was off limits and even if everyone was not comfortable answering the questions, we would have insight about what we want to know about each other. I had plenty of questions I knew I shouldn't ask. That therapist didn't know Mama. Charlene was still my mother, and she'd shut me down real quick. We never went back. We moved forward as if nothing happened. Deep inside, we knew that acknowledging all of our pain and trauma would not resolve the situation without the proper commitment that no one was truly ready to do.

I reluctantly sat beside her on the sofa, casually resting my feet on the top of the cushion, and prepared to listen to what I internally referred to as "inmate story-time." She handed me my letter and began reading hers and Dad's out loud.

Dear Mama,

First off, I know you wrote all the letters. I appreciate the thought, but you don't have to write for them. I'll just wait for them to come around and write to me when they are ready. How is life treating you? I hope you and Dad are OK. With the wedding on hold right now because of the trouble I am in; I hope you're not too stressed out. For myself, I got a new cell. I know you're worried about me. I been working out and I have an eight-pack now. When I get out, all the ladies will be on me. I am going to tone my body up and add more detail with the cuts. LMAO, I know you don't care, but I just want you to know I am OK in here and I am taking it one day at a time. I hate that I am putting you through this, but know that I am sorry, and I love you.

P.S. Big Mama would be happy to know that I have been reading the bible. No matter what goes down in my life I know Luke 15:7 "I say to you that likewise there will be more joy in heaven over one sinner who repents than over ninety-nine just persons who need no repentance."

In the Meantime,
Samson

After a short pause, she folded her letter and pulled out the one for my father. I guess she figured that as his wife, she had the right to read both. Edmond didn't mind either way. He consistently secluded himself in the back house. Something weighed heavily on him, though he remained silent about it. Maybe it was guilt, especially since he was more concerned with the affairs of Charles Simmons than the well-being of his only son. But it wasn't my problem, and I was happy to keep it that way.

Dear Pops,

How are you? I still haven't heard from you, and I am feeling like I might not. Considering I am in here because of you, I expected to get some kind of response. For now, I will live with Mama being the only one to respond. For myself, I believe I am fine. I wish I didn't have to be here. I thought you would have pulled some strings by now and got me out. You say that you were in that life, but I am still stuck in here. I am a little worried about Mama because she can be a stress case. I told her there is nothing to worry about. Tell her I am fine. I believe San Quentin is a lot easier to deal with than Alameda County Jail. I fought a lot there for many reasons I didn't get or understand. Plus, the guards act like bitches!

I'm holding my head up and not letting them see my weakness, but I can't front. I am a little scared. Remember the girl you caught me with at the house? Well, she wrote to me once, which was cool, but none of my so-called patnas have reached out and they probably won't be at my court date, but I know you will come through and get me outta this place. The longer I am down, the more I learn not to stress.

I replay that night over and over in my head and I wouldn't have done it any different. I feel like a man now. I no longer have anything to prove.

In the Meantime,
Samson

Mama took the letters and held them to her chest, like hugging Samson. She drew in a deep, steadying breath and lingered in a moment of thought. I waited, watching to see if she was going to have another crying spell, which meant I'd have to comfort her. But, surprisingly, she didn't. Sadly, she was becoming more comfortable with the thought that he may be in there for a long time.

My parents spent the first two weeks after Samson was arrested—the day of Elijah's funeral—selecting the best lawyer to handle the case. Our family had not been in this type of legal trouble before. To be honest, we didn't trust that any of the qualified candidates truly had Samson's best interest at heart. However, my father insisted on using Michael Flemming. From what I overheard him discussing with Mama, he was affordable. Despite his youth and limited experience, he was reputed to be a beast in the courtroom, he had the fire under him with the will to take on the world.

In truth, a significant portion of my anger and resentment towards my brother stemmed from the fact that he willingly became another statistic. It was already a struggle when I was away at school and people learned of my Oakland origins. I was consistently met with negativity, classmates offering unsolicited "warnings" about the city's supposed dangers and rising crime rates. And then my brother, who had the privilege of a well-mannered, middle-class upbringing, seemed to embody the very image they had conjured. I knew, deep down, that his poor choices didn't reflect his true character or our family. But did that even matter? Did anyone care that he was intelligent and educated? Did they care that he was extremely charismatic and charming? I don't think so. I believe that, in the eyes of the world, actions reign supreme. Actions are the sole measure of character. Whether those actions are made under duress, the influence of a substance or plain immaturity, to the world, what you do, is who you are.

The experience of college forced me to challenge my own rules of understanding. I didn't want to admit it, but I was ashamed of Samson. I knew his actions would make people judge me. A young, Black college girl from Oakland with a brother in prison, just screamed "ghetto."

> Dear Lil Sis (Big Head),
>
> I can't front with you... It is killing me that you haven't written me back. I don't know what I did. I know I let you down and you always told me to stay out the way, but you know I had to do what I had to do. One day when I am out, I'll share with you the full story of what went down, and you may see things a little differently. You know sometimes I do get scared here. I am literally in here with a bunch of grown ass men. The first night I remember being hella nervous and scared. It really dawned on me that night that I had messed up and to be honest with you, I cried. But if you ever bring that up, I'll deny it. But anyway, I think about the times when I was disrespectful to Mama and Pops and in a way, I feel like all of this is punishment for all my actions.
>
> In county, there were 30 inmates with one toilet. Can you imagine having to wait and taking a shit in front of a bunch of strangers? Makes me really thankful for what I had. Having to wear county clothes and having a diet consisting of peanut butter and jelly sandwiches, cookies, milk, and an apple. You know I was up in there, starving! Sis, I have never been more violated in my life. Imagine having to squat and cough, standing in a line bucket naked, open mouth, lift arm, balls pulled back. Not something you get used to. But your bro is good.
>
> I hope you write back this time. I guess I'll keep writing until you do.
>
> > In the Meantime,
> > Samson

***

The knocking on my passenger-side window startled me out of my trance.

"Are you coming inside?" Daddy requested, hunched down, peering through the fogged-up passenger side window. Per usual, he was dressed in run-down house shoes and his antique robe.

"Yes, Daddy, I'm coming in. I'll get out in a second." I turned off the ignition.

He hesitated a moment before retiring back into the house. He kept a watchful eye out, at all times, to monitor the activity in the community. He knew everyone who was coming in and leaving out. I could not come and go without him escorting me into the house and back out to the car. After Calvin was murdered, the streets kept talking. People knew Samson went down for it and that most likely my dad had something to do with it. There were still individuals that were not happy about it. Some drove by the house or called incessantly, leaving death threats on the answering machine. Nothing came of it for the most part. The better part of the community was on our side, supporting us to keep most of it at bay. Once you have been conditioned to watching your back and being vigilant in the community, it never goes away. Daddy kept his *Glock* locked and loaded for anyone who felt *froggy*.

Deep breath in, deep breath out. I engaged in one final series of deliberate breathing exercises, attempting to steady my nerves. The air was unexpectedly frigid, and I'd left my coat at home, unprepared for the swift arrival of the fog. I hustled up to the front door, anxious not to keep Daddy waiting. *Definitely needed a coat!* I entered without a greeting, instinctively making my first stop to the restroom, a ritual I followed upon entering any building. The frequency of using the restroom increased more and more. The news of my pregnancy remained a closely guarded secret, unshared with the outside world. I had yet to arrive at a firm decision regarding its disclosure, even on social media. The relentless ticking of an internal clock reminded me I still possessed the power of choice. Or perhaps that was just a convenient delusion, a way to avoid confronting the inevitable. Having experienced a miscarriage in the past, I knew it would be irresponsible to willingly terminate another pregnancy, especially knowing how much I desired a child. It'd probably mess up my chances of ever becoming a mother. I was simply not prepared to face the full weight of the situation.

My mother tapped lightly on the bathroom door. "Debra, you in there?"

"Yeah Mom, I'll be right out in a second." I flushed the toilet and cleaned my hands.

"Meet me and your father in the living room."

"I got you. I'm coming out now." I wanted to give her a moment to move away from the door and get settled, so I took my time.

Both my mother and father were seated next to each other on the large family couch. I loved seeing them in love. They looked good sitting there together, like Ossie Davis and Ruby Dee, happy and connected. Daddy had his hand placed lovingly on Mama's lap.

"Sit down, Baby Girl." My daddy motioned me to sit across from them in the love seat.

"We heard back from Mr. Flemming about the update on Samson's case," Mama started. "He has a release date. He will be out in one month! Just in time for the holidays." She lit up with pure joy and excitement, announcing it. Almost like she was hearing the news for the first time again.

My father, on-the-other-hand, did not have the look of joy on his face. It was more indifferent. "Yeah, he is getting out."

"Isn't this great, Debra? This is what we have been praying for. My baby is going to get out of that awful place." The question was obviously rhetorical. She was not concerned with my response. "We are going to plan a special homecoming for him," she didn't even look to acknowledge me not speaking. "We will go all in. Daddy can barbecue. I am sure he will want all of my favorites. Daddy will pick him up because I'll be way too emotional."

"Mama! Breathe. It's going to be good. I'm happy you're getting your favorite child back, but take a breath."

"Debra, don't do that. This is a blessing, and he has been gone from us for too long. He will need all of us more than ever! That means you will have to step up too and come around more." This time, she paused for a moment for me to comprehend her statement. "Don't think I haven't noticed you have been M.I.A. lately."

"Mama, you don't need anything from me. And you certainly don't need to overwork yourself. He will be fine. If he made it all this time in there, he will be alright." I responded nonchalantly.

"Don't be insensitive, Debra! Your brother went in there physically at twenty, and he is coming out mentally at twenty. There is a lot that he has missed and will need. Why are you not more excited about this? I just knew you would love the idea of your big brother coming home."

"What could he possibly need? A job? A place to stay? You continue to focus on *his* needs, and I have been here, in the flesh, for the past twelve years! Have you called and checked on me?" I questioned, tip-toeing near an invisible boundary.

"Debra, you're not a child. You're a grown woman. A married woman and Derrick's concern, for that matter!" Charlene hissed.

"Mama, stop playing. You don't even like Derrick."

"I've never told you I don't like him. I barely know the man and y'all have been married five years. He rarely comes around here to spend time with us. Since you married the man, you act like we don't exist. Ain't that right, Babe?"

"Don't put me in it." Daddy said, leaning back and grabbing the remote. "I told Debra the first time she brought him around; I told her what kind of guy he was. I saw too much of myself in him and to be careful with her heart. Didn't I?"

"Yeah Daddy, you did. What y'all want me to say?"

"Baby Girl, we don't want you to say anything. You made your choice and married the man. Now we just got to get to know him so we can decide whether we truly like him or not." Daddy chuckled to himself. "It's good y'all don't have any kids yet because that always tends to complicate things. Although your mother and I love you and Samson," he cleared his throat, "if we were to do it differently, we would have waited to have you until we were more mature and ready to handle all that came with becoming parents."

"There is no right time for babies," Mama interrupted, "there's no, *when the time is right*... it's just when the Lord blesses. He knows it is right because he allows it and knows that you will be able to handle all that comes with it." She took Daddy's hand, held it tightly against her chest, and gently kissed it.

"All that your mom and I went through could have been avoided. And look at us now, planning a homecoming celebration for your knucklehead brother. At least y'all know he didn't get it from me!" he said sarcastically, breaking out into laughter.

"You got one more time, babe, to throw a jab. Now you raised the boy, so he got all of your ways!" Charlene rebutted.

"Seriously, Baby Girl," Daddy started, "what your mom means is, we gotta stick together when Samson gets out. We need to be strong as a family. Not everyone's gonna be happy he's coming home. We want him safe. We need him to know we're here for him, so he doesn't go back to his old ways." He tried to reassure me, then paused, like he always did, to make sure I got it. He was always good at keeping things calm.

If Samson would be that stupid, as to get out of prison, and return right back to the very thing that got him locked up in the first place, he would very well deserve to rot in prison. My concern was not for him or *his* issues. My parents should be grateful I am here and put their focus on the things within their control.

"Whatever you need me to do, I'll do it." I said, trying to put her mind at ease.

"Great!" Charlene chimed in. "I'm gonna need you to help with the food and to let his friends know. I'll handle the invites, decorations, music, tables, and chairs." She jumped up to grab her notebook from the table. "And your dad's gonna do the barbecue." She patted his leg. "I want this to be perfect. Everyone's invited to show my baby some love."

I started thinking, this party could actually be good. It'd give Mama practice to prepare for the baby shower she may need to plan in a few months. So, I figured, no more waiting. I was just gonna say what I really needed to say.

"Mommy and Daddy, I'm pregnant."

For a second, nobody said anything. Daddy looked confused at first, but then he smiled. Charlene was beaming with joy.

"Oh, my Lord! My first grandbaby." She hopped up and grabbed me, hugging me tightly. "This is great news; I'm so happy for you!"

Right then, I felt torn. I'd actually created a special moment between us, yet I found myself struggling to share in her joy.

"It is and..." I hesitated.

"I've been waiting for this day," Mama continued, filling the quiet space. "I never wanted to burden you, so I kept my thoughts to myself. With Samson being locked up, I somewhat gave up hope. But God! He is looking down on our family. He knows the void left after Big Mama. This is a full circle moment." Tears glistened in the corners of her eyes. "God's bringing my son home and blessing us with a baby."

"So, Baby Girl, how are you really doing?" Daddy asked. "I'm getting the feeling you're not exactly thrilled about this news." He always knew how to see right through me.

"I'm not. I don't know if I'm going to keep it."

"What do you mean? This is a blessing. If God is doing this, you can't step in *His* way. You know your odds of getting pregnant?"

"I know, Mama, but things are not great with Derrick. We might be getting a divorce!"

"And what does that have to do with the baby? You have us!" she reminded me.

"Do I? With Samson coming home, you will be focused on him, and I dare not have a newborn around a criminal."

"Is that what you think about your brother?"

"Let's be honest. Samson never has made good decisions. He murdered his own father, regardless of if he knew he was or not, and who knows how many others and I am supposed to be comfortable bringing my baby around him? The timing is not right."

"What has gotten into you, Debra?" Charlene demanded. "That's your brother! The one that always looked out for you growing up to make sure you were protected. He made sure that nobody messed with his little sister. Do you think he would harm the baby?"

"I don't know what he might do, but I can't put it past him. There are twelve unaccounted years of animalistic behavior that I am certain he adopted in that place to survive. It doesn't just leave you!"

"Debra, I can't believe you. You're so selfish and bitter. Have you considered anyone else outside of yourself?" Mama paced back and forth with her hands on her face in disbelief.

"Charlene, baby, why don't you start dinner? I need to talk to Debra for a minute." He got up and rubbed her back gently, whispering something in her ear, and she reluctantly turned and left to the kitchen.

"Debra, what's going on with you and Derrick? Why are you talking divorce all of a sudden? Is he hurting you?" Daddy looked me dead in the eye, with a look that demanded complete honesty.

I didn't say a word. I just sat there. He asked me again, just in case I didn't hear him the first time. I dropped my head and started sobbing. "No, Daddy." I forced out, keeping my head down in shame.

"Then what is it? What's going on?"

"I should have known better. You told me and I didn't listen. I thought I knew enough for myself. I honestly thought you were just being overprotective and didn't want me to find happiness."

"Oh sweetheart. You know I am always going to look out for you, and I only want the best for you."

"I know, Daddy, but I really thought he was different. He promised me he'd love me and take care of me. He swore he'd never cheat. But it is not the cheating that I have an issue with, he got another woman pregnant knowing it was difficult for me to do so. It feels like I'm living your life all over again."

"Hold on a sec, let's not go down the victim road, okay? You know I love you and I'm always gonna be straight with you. Whatever your mother and I did, we were two adults making choices we thought were right then. Sometimes we give people too much virtue. We think that everyone has this ability to be stronger than their flesh at all times. But we're all flawed. We do our best, try to be better every day, but we mess up. You mess up too. And that's okay, just do better. You hear me?"

I glanced up at him and wiped my eyes, trying to clear them as he kept talking.

"You knew what you were getting into. He was exactly who you thought he was, and you expected him to be something different. You were fine with it when he was all smooth-talking and getting you in bed. But you keep everything from us anyway, so whatever's going on over there is y'all business. Just don't let our grandbaby suffer for your poor judgment. Let God decide. You know that the doctors said you can't carry a baby, so let God have the final say. If you're able to carry this child to term, then God is presenting you with an opportunity for a fresh start, with or without your husband. But you're gonna have to work harder to be your best every day."

This was exactly why I loved him. He had such wisdom and

always knew how to keep things in the right perspective—with love and kindness. "Thanks, Daddy."

"Look, I'm not saying I'm perfect; I've made my mistakes. But the minute I knew I was going to be a dad, something changed for me. And even though I had my doubts about Samson, I stayed with your mom because I knew I'd put her through a lot. I'm not telling you to stay with Derrick, that's your call. But you need to figure out why he's doing what he's doing. There's a reason he's stepped out and stayed away. Can you fix it? Are you willing to try? Is your marriage worth saving? Those are questions you gotta answer yourself. Whatever you decide, we're here for you."

I hugged Daddy tightly. If Derrick was like him, we might have a chance.

CHAPTER 4

Week 2

Monday Afternoon

The lunch bell boomed in my ear; signaling the halfway point of my day. My throat felt like sandpaper, and my stomach was rumbling audibly, a fact that was only partially masked by the persistent ringing in my ear. It was College Day, and I'd chosen to wear my U.C. Riverside sweatshirt, a vibrant display of blue and gold featuring Scotty the Bear, paired with my favorite blue mom jeans. Being a curvy woman, I preferred loose-fitting attire, hoping to avoid any unwanted attention from the students. My stomach protruded slightly over my belt, and I'd discreetly adjusted it to accommodate the subtle expansion. Though my degree wasn't from Riverside, I still kept all my gear, for sentimental reasons. Oddly, I loved the bear more than the gator and was not ashamed of it. Still, my bachelor's degree in sociology from San Francisco State hung proudly on my wall, a constant reminder of the unexpected and drastic turns my life had taken.

Again, the ringing exploded in my ear, releasing the wave of students racing to the lunch line. This Monday felt agonizingly slow. The news of Samson's release was definitely contributing to the nausea I felt creeping in. My earlier optimism about the morning sickness subsiding was rapidly fading. I had neglected my usual routine of drinking water and snacking on almonds, a practice that typically kept my stomach settled. It must have been something in the air. Students flooded my office more frequently than usual to talk. My stomach turned. I pushed myself up slowly, planning a sprint to the restroom. But just as I got to my feet...

"Mrs. Covington, can I talk to you for a second?"

I turned around and saw one of my students sitting in the chair by my office. He seemed kind of embarrassed.

"Are you okay, Redd?" I asked, concerned.

"Not exactly. I got kicked out of class again."

"It's lunchtime. Where have you been since you got kicked out?" I felt my insides holding on by a thread. "Give me one second, sweetheart." I quickly made my way to the nearest private faculty restroom, seeking the relief my stomach demanded. Since I'd been throwing up way more than I wanted, I'd started keeping a travel toothbrush and toothpaste at work. I freshened up and returned to my office, feeling slightly better. Redd was still sitting there, his backpack resting between his legs.

"Are you okay, Mrs. Covington? I can always come back."

"I'm alright, Redd." I reassured him. "Thank you for your concern, but you're here now, so you might as well spit it out. What's going on?"

"My parents are fighting again."

"And does their fighting involve you?" I questioned.

"Yes. They're still unhappy with my decision."

I'm pretty sure I was just staring at Redd with a blank look, like, *Okay, and what's your point?* The students were well aware of my straightforward approach. They understood that my office was not a place for games. I was not their get-out-of-class-free card. If they came to me, they needed to be ready to talk and answer every single question. When they were straightforward, it saved me the trouble of pulling information out of them.

"My dad always blames Mom for how I am. He wants me to be more 'girly' and won't even call me *Redd*. But Mom's not much better. She avoids looking at me, like, ever."

"How does this translate to you getting kicked out of class?" I asked, trying to get to the point. "How is calling Ms. Hansen *a dumb bitch* connected to your parents' arguing? You know, she reached out to me and explained the whole thing."

"Well... it doesn't."

"So why are you *here*, Redd? Your mom and dad fighting is nothing new. They've been at odds regarding your behavior and decisions since you started here in the ninth grade. They either want credit for the good or blame each other for the bad. It hasn't bothered you up to this point. *Why are you here?*" I asked again for emphasis.

"You know, Mrs. Covington, that's why I like you. You don't show any favoritism and just keep it real. I just wanted to practice my sob story for Ms. Hansen. We have a re-entry meeting later today so I can return to class. Is it believable?"

"Absolutely not! But I wouldn't be surprised if it works. You need to practice apologizing. Get out of my office and close the door behind you!"

"Alright Mrs. C, I'll holla at ya later when I get kicked out of Mr. Humphrey's class. I don't feel like doing math today."

"Don't do it, Redd! I'll call ya daddy, mama, ya granny, and ya uncle. Don't play with me!"

"Damn Mrs. C, you don't have to do all that. I'll go to class!"

I couldn't help but smile once Redd was out of sight. He was one of my "special" students, one I felt particularly protective of. During the first week of his freshmen year, he was a regular in my office. High school was a tough adjustment for him, especially with everyone having to switch from calling him Ronisha to Redd. His parents weren't making it any easier, either. They were giving him and the school a really hard time about changing his name in the system and using he/him pronouns. We connected by accident. I was out patrolling the hallways one day and I noticed him arguing with his science teacher. He wouldn't give up his phone when she asked. And, being me, I just had to intervene.

I observed Redd frequently in the hallways and made a conscious effort to simply speak and leave it at that. Just to let him know I *saw* him. This seemingly small gesture fostered an unspoken connection, which resulted in me being called upon whenever issues arose. Unlike some of the other teachers, I engaged in meaningful conversations with Redd to gain insight into his experiences on campus. And it felt good to know that he was also looking out for me. I didn't have to worry about any student giving me a hard time. Not with Redd around. I'd say, "Thanks Redd, but I got this! I'm from East Oakland." The students got a kick out of that, and they really left me alone.

I powered on my laptop, and the screen flooded with emails and chat notifications from students, parents, and, of course, Ms. Hansen. Honestly, I was not in the mood. Just as I was about to close everything, I saw an urgent email from the principal. I reluctantly clicked it open, knowing instinctively it wasn't going to be good. Urgent emails always carried the weight of a prime-time news bulletin, laden with a tragic backstory and a disheartening resolution.

The email's subject line was: "SALISHA COBBS STILL MISSING!"

It just broke my heart knowing one of my students was missing. Out there on the streets, probably taken by some sex trafficker. I didn't want to jump to conclusions, but all the signs were there. Our Black girls are so susceptible to these dangers. First, Salisha was hanging with a new group of girls, then she was wearing more makeup and revealing clothes, then skipping school. Rumors circulated about an older boyfriend, with frequent overnight stays at his apartment. Her parents, tragically, had failed to intervene. And now she has been reported missing. It was going on the 5th day since her disappearance, and I was praying daily for a positive outcome.

I've heard so many stories from my students about what it's

like to be a teenager today; that has instilled a deep hesitation within me about bringing a child into this world. I see it every day at school. Growing up isn't what it used to be. Sure, having a child is a beautiful thing, but there's so much pain, so much you can't protect them from. Working at Fremont High School was a constant reminder of the endless risks. Three weeks ago, we had a shooting outside. We locked down, but not one parent showed up. It was like it was normal. Everyone was back the next day, like nothing happened. Just another day.

Mr. Warren wanted all staff members to know that the school was doing everything in its power to support her return. He advised all teachers to report any and all information shared by students to him immediately. In addition, school therapists were on standby for any students that needed a check-in. I appreciated Mr. Warren's leadership. He was one of the few black male principals working in the Oakland Public School District. Who am I kidding? He was one of the few black male principals PERIOD! It felt good knowing he was compassionate and well respected by the entire staff. His presence made a huge difference on campus as well. Suspensions were down, student academic performance was up, and as a school, we were building a reputation for more than sports.

"Hey beautiful. What's got you looking so down? It is a beautiful day above ground." I was so lost in that email, I didn't even hear someone come in. It was Mr. Earl, the school custodian, who was known for letting himself in to spark up unsolicited small talk.

"Hey Mr. Earl. You know how it is," I said, throwing my hands up. I never really knew what he was after, so I just tried to be nice. Frankly, he made me very uneasy. I mean, he was a bit creepy. I would never hear him coming and *poof,* he would be there. He'd just appear out of nowhere, saying these weird, 1970's undercover pickup lines. They made me feel uncomfortable, yet they weren't overtly offensive enough to justify filing a complaint.

"As the sun is shining," he declared, peering out the window, "so is your beauty." He abruptly turned to me, his eyes locking with mine, "Uh… is that husband of yours treating you right? 'Cause, you know, if he ain't doing his job, I can come and take out the trash!" He let out an unsettling chuckle and some other indecipherable sounds. Then, he proceeded to replace the wastebasket liner to justify why he was in my office, even though it was empty.

"Thank you, Mr. Earl. We are good."

"You know I always have to come in here and check on my girl," he flashed another quick smile. "I saw you rush off to the bathroom earlier. You alright? You're looking a little under the weather." His words felt invasive and his observations too personal.

"I'm fine, Mr. Earl. It was probably something I ate that didn't agree with me. I'll be okay."

"Now you know I was not born yesterday, and I have been around the block a few times. I know a pregnant woman when I see one."

"Shhh. Mr. Earl! I don't need this office in my business!"

"So, you are?"

"Well, it's complicated. But, um, I think I'd rather not talk about it right now."

He must have misunderstood me because he pulled up a chair. He set the trash bag down on the floor and leaned in.

"Listen, whatever you're thinking, just know that a baby is a blessing. I see how you are with these kids every day, giving them your all. That little one you're carrying is going to have all that and more. Don't let your husband make you second-guess yourself or your own strength."

I don't know how he read me. I thought I was masking things, but I was glass. I tried to hold it together, but I couldn't.

"You know, men, we don't always get it right. Sometimes we take out our frustrations on the women we care about. I know; I've messed up plenty of times myself. I'm sixty-three, and after two failed marriages, you'd think I'd have learned by now, but here I am. Still hoping to find that special someone. Don't let him take away your peace. You're a beautiful, smart woman. He'll either wake up or miss out."

I couldn't even interject at this point. My sobs continued. I thought I was all cried out from the intervention with my dad over the weekend. Mr. Earl offered me a tissue from the box on my desk and proceeded with his impromptu counseling session.

"I wish that we men would learn things faster and not put all the pressure on you women. Now, all women ain't as put together as you and some can be worthy of what they get. We put y'all through too much while placing the blame on ya in the process. So, on behalf of your husband, I want to say sorry. Sorry for not seeing you, hearing you, loving you the way he should have. Oh, what I would give to say those words to my exes." Mr. Earl finally took a breath and gazed at the ceiling, shaking his head in disbelief.

The bell sounded, startling us both. I wiped my face, cleared my throat, and mustered up enough energy to respond.

"Thank you." It was all I had and all that needed to be said.

He just nodded, like he got it. Picked up the trash bag, and left. I don't know, maybe it was just me, but it felt like God had sent two people to give me a little pep talk. I was still confused about what it all meant, what I was supposed to do, but I felt like someone was watching out for me. I wrestled internally with the clarity of the message, specifically whether I should Derrick another chance. A growing conviction told me he had reached his limit, and that in my next chapter, I would have to walk alone.

Tap, Tap, Tap.

"Come in."

"Hola, Señora C."

"Hi Kelman. Come in and have a seat. Do you have your pass?"

"Sí. It's right here." He showed me his hall pass and sat down across from me.

"So how are you? ¿Cómo estás? How are you adjusting?"

"It's good. I like this school. People are nice. Me gusta aquí."

"I want to speak with you about your transcript and grades. We need to make sure you're placed in the correct classes next semester so there are no problems with graduation. Since we didn't have your records right away, we placed you in 12th grade classes. ¿Cómo van las clases?"

"Mis clases son buenas. I don't like math class because it is too loud. The kids don't listen to Señor Chan. It's hard to learn when all the students are playing around."

"I know, but it will hopefully get better. You can also go to Mr. Chan's office hours after school."

"I will. I just want to graduate and make my family proud. Since mi papá opened up the coffee and cigar bar last year, business has been good. We will be able to bring the rest of the family over. I'll be the first graduate in my family and the first to do it in America."

"What an honor! You don't have to worry. We will get you across that stage."

"I really hope so. My family's done so much to give us a good life, and I just want to do my part, you know? I really want to make them proud. My mom's been really sick, and I think graduating would really cheer her up. It's good that she's right upstairs from the store, so Papá can take care of her whenever he needs to."

"Oh no, is she alright?" I don't know why I asked that, since he just said she was sick. But, I believe he understood my deeper concern.

"Right now, she's okay, thankfully, but things could still get really bad. We came here from República Dominicana to get medical care and treatment. I'm going to do everything I can for her, because I know that's what she'd want."

"You're so strong, and I'm very proud of you. You're a great student, and you will definitely make it across that stage."

"Señora C, I really appreciate you. Since I first came, you have always been really kind to me, like a second mother. I feel like I can come and talk to you about anything. I'm sure your kids are blessed to have you."

"Oh, thank you, but I don't have any kids."

"¿Por qué no?"

"Umm... well... I want them for sure, but I just haven't been able to have them."

"When you do, you will be an amazing mom! All the kids here love you. You're pretty much everyone's favorite."

My face flushed. Truthfully, it hadn't truly registered the extent to which I impacted the students. I knew we had a connection, sure, and I got along well with them, but I never considered the depth of it, how it resonated within their personal lives. I felt tears coming on again, and I knew I had to get Kelman to leave.

"Alright, Kelman, I'll check in with you again next week. I don't want you missing too much of Mr. Chan's class, though. Make sure you talk to him about staying after school for office hours."

"Sure thing, Señora C." He got up and pushed in the chair he was seated in. He was such a respectful and honorable young man. Just before leaving, he turned back around, "Is that your husband in the photo?"

I looked at the photo. "It is." I forgot he was on full display, on my desk, right next to the stapler. The picture was taken during happier times.

"I thought I recognized him the other day when he came into the coffee shop. I wasn't sure though, because he was there with another woman. They were kind of close. After seeing this photo, I am sure it was him."

"It was probably his sister." I suggested.

"I don't think he would be close to his sister like that."

"Then maybe it was someone else." I offered, though I wasn't entirely sure why I felt the need to convince Kelman. It was, undeniably, him. My own embarrassment fueled the denial. Knowing of his indiscretions was one matter, but having them revealed to the students was another story.

"No offense, Señora C, but I know it was him. His name is Derrick, ¿cierto?"

"Yes, his name is Derrick. Thank you, Kelman, for letting me know. I'll talk to him tonight."

"I just wanted you to know because I don't want you to get hurt. They come in there often."

"Oh, really?"

"Yes. They are pretty much regulars. Her name is Tatiana, she used to work there, but not anymore."

I could feel my stomach beginning to turn upside down. I didn't need this information now, and certainly not from a seventeen-year-old student. "Thanks for looking out, Kel. I really appreciate it. Now get back to class. Here is your pass."

"Alright Señora C, see you later."

CHAPTER 5

Week 2
Wednesday Early-Evening

I was filled with anxiety and apprehension, this time returning to our session with Laura. The week had been eerily calm because, quite frankly, we had not been communicating. No adjectives, verbs, nouns, or syllables—no exchanges. I decided not to bring up "the tea" Kelman shared with me. I figured I would hold it until it would be needed—keep it in my pocket for a rainy day.

Derrick isolated himself, giving me the silent treatment. I welcomed it. The absence of his complaints brought me peace. The spark was gone from our relationship, now a fragile flame threatening to extinguish. He used to tell me how unhappy he was, how I fell short as a wife, how he wanted to escape. The silence was a break from that negativity. I wondered why he still came home each night. If Tatiana was truly where he wanted to be, why didn't he just go?

"I apologize, I'm a bit late, a session ran over," Laura said, rushing in, slightly breathless and with disheveled hair, notepad in hand. "I'll make up the time. Let's get started." She looked up and waited for our energy or excitement, and neither one of us had much to give her. "I can't help but notice the distance between you both," Laura remarked, pausing to steady herself. "Before we review the homework, Debra, perhaps you could tell me why you're sitting so far from Derrick?"

Looking at the space between us, I cleared my throat to speak. I came prepared for all the heat and all the smoke. I knew the air would soon be thick with tension, a fiery exchange. This was going to be a full-blown explosion. I understood I needed to abandon all pretense and dive in headfirst. No more sugarcoating things to maintain his happiness. With Laura as a mediator, I could finally unleash the emotions I'd been suppressing.

"Well... We have not been talking. Derrick is distant and I'm not sure if it is worth it anymore."

"When you say worth it, what do you mean?" Laura poked to pull more out of me.

"Basically, I'm not seeing any progress from the counseling. I'm starting to wonder if it's even worth continuing, either the therapy or the marriage itself," I stated plainly.

"We've just started. It's only been one session. We haven't even gotten to the real work yet."

"Exactly! I don't know if the work is worth it!" I retorted, hoping she would accept it and move on.

"So, you want a divorce?" Derrick asked, sitting up abruptly, finally speaking. "It sounds like you're done with me, which is news to me. I don't know who you've been talking to, but your little friends can't keep a man, so I hope you're not listening to them?" He stared at me, waiting for a response.

His tone had a definite attitude. "What I'm saying is, you only bother with things that serve your own interests. *And... as cliché as it might sound, I can do bad all by myself!*" I deliberately ignored his slick comment about my friends, even though they've been telling me to leave him for ages.

"Debra, let's pause for a second and talk about something important. Why did you decide to marry Derrick? What was it about him that you saw then, that seems to be different now?"

"When we first met, things were explosive. We couldn't keep our hands off of each other. We were always together. He was so loving, in a way that felt completely new to me." I said, choosing my words carefully. My feelings were all jumbled, but she was trying to steer me towards a better memory, despite the tension. "Maybe that doesn't mean much, as I haven't had many relationships. But now, he is cold and mean. He complains about everything and spends all day at work or wherever he goes during the day. He is unfaithful and don't get me started on his drinking..." I rolled my eyes as I let Laura interrupt.

"We could keep going with that list, but I want to shift gears. What does Derrick need that you haven't been giving him, in your opinion?"

I hesitated. It felt like Laura was taking his side. *Was Laura implying that I was responsible for his cheating? I wanted to trust her, to avoid rushing to judgment.* "To be honest," I admitted, "I'm not giving him anything right now. He doesn't deserve it, not after everything."

"If you've already given up on the marriage, how do you expect it to improve? Who's going to do the work if you're not even trying?" she asked, her eyes searching mine, as if anticipating me dodging the question.

"How do I show up if I am there alone?"

"You just do! And you wait for him to meet you there. If he doesn't decide to meet you, then you no longer have a decision to make. The only decision at this moment is showing up. Likewise, it is the same for him."

Laura turned to Derrick. "Derrick, why are *you* here?"

"I don't want to lose my wife." He responded immediately, "She gets on my nerves, but I swear I love her. For real. I say shit to her to get her off my back and leave me alone, but I don't mean no harm." He practically shouted, clenching his hands together and staring intensely at me.

If this was his form of an apology, he was going to have to do much better.

"Good. We have a starting point. With willingness, we can move forward. So, let's get to the homework. Derrick, I'll start with you." Laura was now fully in her therapist mode.

He shifted in his seat, rubbing his hands together, and tilted his head. I knew the bullshit was coming. "I got caught up this week and didn't get a chance to do it. But I can do it now if you give me a minute."

"For this process to work, you need to trust it and come prepared. That means doing the assigned activities and tasks before we meet."

"I do understand, and I apologize. I'll do better."

I glanced at Derrick in disbelief. *Who did he think he was foolin'?* He was laying it on thick with the charm, and I knew it was an act. I wouldn't fall for it, but I kept my thoughts to myself to avoid seeming disengaged.

"Derrick, this isn't for my benefit. You need to find value in this work to see any progress. I'm not interested in being convinced," Laura pointed out. It was impressive how quickly she'd seen through his bullshit, just like I had, *and* she has only known him for two weeks.

"Debra, did you do the homework?"

"I did."

"So, let's start with you. I am coming back to you Derrick, so you're not off the hook. Think about your answers, but listen to your wife as well."

"Okay, five things I love about Derrick… First, he's hardworking. He's not lazy at all. He works constantly, provides for us, and takes care of the house. He even says I wouldn't have to work if it were up to him, which I appreciate." Sharing that made me smile. "Second, he's so romantic. He loves to surprise me with flowers, give me massages out of the blue, and make sure I get time for myself. Sometimes I come home and the laundry's done; he tells me to sit down, rubs my feet, plays my favorite music, lights candles, and has dinner ready. Third, he genuinely takes care of me. He meets my needs, and he's a great lover. Fourth, he's so spontaneous and fun when things are good. There's never a dull moment. He always makes me laugh. And fifth, he's very handsome. He's a very attractive man, and he takes care of himself. I like that a lot." I glanced over at Derrick, his chest poked out, showing all 32 of his teeth. He was definitely feeling himself, a reminder of what we once had.

"That's helpful, Debra. Now, how do you support those things you mentioned?" Sensing my hesitation, Laura rephrased. "You've named five wonderful qualities, but how do you nurture or encourage Derrick to keep embodying them?"

I never considered what she was asking. It hadn't occurred to me that I wasn't showing appreciation for the things he did, let alone encouraging him. "I... I... I guess I've neglected that part of our relationship," I admitted. "There's definitely more that I can do, like acknowledging when he is doing those things, so he knows I see it and appreciate it. I can also be more generous with compliments and praise."

"I'd really appreciate that." Derrick added.

"See, we're already making progress. Let's not delay. Tell him what you appreciate about him now. This is the first step in strengthening your bond. If you practice this when it's hard, it'll become natural when things are easy."

I faced Derrick, unprepared. All I could picture was him with Tatiana. I was still wrestling with if the relationship was worth saving, but I made a promise to myself to try. "Derrick," I began hesitantly, "you're an amazing man. You've been there for me in ways I can't even begin to describe, and it's meant the world to me. You're my best friend, and I love you." I paused, fighting back tears, and nervously fiddled with my bracelet, my eyes fixed on the floor. I couldn't shake the feeling that I was being dishonest.

"I see you're struggling and want to stop, but don't close off. There's more you need to say. Keep talking," Laura encouraged.

I continued, "I also want to say that I truly enjoy spending time with you. Your gentle spirit brings me peace and calms my anxieties. You're incredibly hardworking and provide so well for our family. I admire your drive and how you pursue your goals. Your growth means a lot to me, and I see how you could be a great influence on those around you."

"There's more you want to say, isn't there? What's stopping you?" Laura inquired.

"I don't know. I feel like I shouldn't have to explain," I said, frustrated because I was the one doing all the work, as usual. I was always the one trying.

"What do you truly want Derrick to understand, that you're not saying aloud?"

"I... I said it! I want him to do right by me!"

"Tell *him*."

"Derrick, I need you to do right by me and stop seeing other women. I don't want a divorce. I love you, and I desperately want to make this work. I'm having our baby, and I expect you to be here, to be a father. But I can't stay if I'm not treated with respect. Becoming a mother is my lifelong dream, and I won't go through another abortion because of our problems!" A heavy weight lifted from me. I took a long, deep breath and let it out.

"Now, how did that feel?" Laura questioned.

"That was hard, but I feel good now. Relieved. How did you know that's what I needed to say?"

"I wasn't sure of the exact words, but I sensed you were holding something back. We tend to carefully select what we say to protect others' feelings, but that often means we're not expressing our real desires. My goal was to create a space for you to speak freely. Derrick needs the opportunity to hear your genuine truth."

Derrick moved closer, taking my hand. He remained silent, his gaze fixed on Laura, anticipating his turn. He squeezed my hand, acknowledging he'd heard me.

"Given that you did not complete the assigned homework, Derrick, I'm asking you to speak directly to Debra. Please express five things you love about her and explain how you intend to cultivate those aspects," Laura directed.

"Baby, I first want to apologize to you for the way that I have been acting. I haven't been talking to you and basically been an asshole and for that I am sorry," he started. "I love everything about you. Literally. Down to the way you sit on the toilet."

I giggled. As I said before, he was fun to be around and kept me laughing.

"Real shit. Laura, I love *this* woman! She knows it. I'm on my bullshit sometimes and I know it. But you're a natural beauty. In real life, you look good with no makeup on, and you go hard for yo' boy! I know you got my back. Even when I don't deserve that shit. You got me! Ain't nothing more I need to say. You will be a phenomenal mom. The way you take care of and love my son is major!" He paused, swallowing hard. "But..." he hesitated again. "If I'm being honest, I don't know if all that is enough anymore. I don't have the motivation to do right by you."

The conversation was about to derail completely; I could feel it. I clenched my lip tightly, and my hand grew increasingly sweaty. After pouring my heart out, it seemed to have made no impact. I held my tongue, determined not to betray my emotions. I couldn't let him see any sign of weakness.

"Baby, I need you to know that I can't be the man of your dreams. I'm not him. I'm fucked up in the head and you keep wanting me to show up as *that man* and I'm gonna let you down every time. I know that now."

The feeling of being his second choice was overwhelming. I tried to ignore his words, but they burrowed deep, dragging me into a spiral of negativity and past traumas. It echoed my childhood, always feeling like an afterthought in Samson's shadow. He was loved and adored, even when he was the thorn in their flesh. I had to fight tooth and nail for attention. Jamel left me pregnant and didn't look back, and now my marriage was crumbling. I had clung to the belief that Derrick was different, ignoring all the red flags. I believed what I desperately wanted to believe, and it led me here, to this painful honesty. Could I blame him for living in his truth? Was it too late for me to find mine?

"Laura, I gotta admit when I met Deb, she had it going on. I mean, her body was bangin'. It was a Friday poetry night at the Air Lounge. She was vibin' with her girls and I had to go over to her and say something. I knew I probably shouldn't have, given my situation, but I couldn't help myself. Her eyes were calling me over to her. We must have talked for ninety minutes right there. We exchanged numbers and talked damn near every day. She told me how she had just moved back to the Bay from Riverside and all the drama that was going on with her family. Her brother getting locked up and even the miscarriage. We connected on a deep level because I had my own family and relationship problems."

"I'm sorry to interrupt," Laura said, "but I think it's important to note that your connection began with shared trauma. What you have is a trauma bond."

"Trauma bond? What's that?" Derrick questioned.

"Trauma bonding occurs as a psychological response to abuse, resulting in an unhealthy attachment. This leads to a dependence on emotional security, which unfortunately perpetuates a cycle of abuse. You two shared traumatic experiences and looked to each other for safety, yet your relationship's foundation became toxic and unstable."

"What makes you think that? I wasn't done talking," Derrick challenged, with a hint of offense in his voice.

"Debra said the relationship started explosively. You also mentioned you were in a 'situation' when you met. This suggests to me that Debra overlooked your circumstances because she was caught up in the intensity and was willing to be involved regardless. Debra, is that accurate?"

"Well damn. I hadn't thought of that. But you're right," I confessed.

"Let me explain what might have happened. Change is inevitable, yet humans fear and resist it. Since you bonded over shared trauma, there's a comfort in knowing you'll always have that to connect you. But when one of you changes or heals, a drift begins. The reasons for staying together fade. One wants growth, the other wants things to stay the same. This creates toxicity because you're no longer in the same emotional space." She paused, letting her words sink in. It made a lot of sense. "Please continue your story, Derrick. I just wanted you to understand how you got here and how to move forward."

"Man, you really got me over here stuck." Derrick said, searching for his place in the story. "So, yeah, I told her about Shayla. We were having problems then. It was cool talking to someone different. She was all over me, so I gave her attention. She liked that. I was also living with my son, DJ, who was eight when I met Deb. They got along for the most part. She was good with him. My baby was a natural. As I said, I was still seeing Shayla on and off, and I liked having both options; I won't lie." He glanced at me, but I gave no reaction. I stayed quiet. "Deb was good, though. She didn't complain. I'd just gotten the electrician gig and was makin' bread. I had my own place and paid my bills. We were good. Things moved fast. I pursued her. Six months in, I proposed. I had to break things off with Shayla, and others, I'll admit. Shayla had already found someone else, so it was easy. Deb and I got married three months later at the courthouse, and we did our thang."

"At what point did things change for you, Derrick?"

"Shayla was cool with me being married, but she got weird about DJ living with us. I think she thought he would get closer to Debra and not feel close to her. Some silly shit. Anyway, she took DJ back after six months into our marriage, meaning I had to go to *her* to see him. We were still on good terms, so I didn't trip. I took advantage of that. Deb made it easy by not asking questions. I always came home and didn't stay out overnight. As long as I came home, I felt I was good. Shay didn't want to get back together; we were just friends. We got along without drama."

Looking back, I realized I hadn't asked questions. Laura was absolutely right. I was content as long as he was there and treated me like a queen. It didn't matter where he went. That changed when I felt like Shayla and DJ became more important. He started avoiding me. He made more excuses why he couldn't do certain things or be around me. The need to have a baby, to keep him from leaving, consumed me. I had a plan to get pregnant. I had this idea of a daughter, believing she'd complete him, complete us. He already had a son; he needed a little princess to be complete. I knew how men adored their daughters. They can't say no. I pulled myself back to the present, wanting to hear the rest of his recollection.

"Things started changing at home. Deb was always irritated, always looking for a fight. We got into this cycle where we'd have these big blow-ups, and then have amazing make-up sex. Not sure if we really made up, but for me, if the sex was good, I was good. I didn't care about the fight. If it ended in me busting a nut, I was good." Derrick chuckled to himself. I did not find it as amusing. "Deb started talking about wanting to have a baby and honestly became obsessed with it. I knew she had a condition that kept her from being able to carry a baby, so I never pressed the issue. *She* did. She got pregnant a couple times, and lost 'em. It was tough. I saw it really affecting her. She lost a lot of weight. The way she looked when we first met, that attraction, it just wasn't the same. I wanted her to be happy. I never pressured her, but I did want a baby. Then she got pregnant *again*, this third time. By then, I'd started seeing Tatiana. I was frustrated at home. She took my mind off things, and we didn't have to talk babies and drama. I was grieving too. Those were my seeds that were not growing. I didn't know if it was my karma, but I also thought something might be wrong with Deb. I knew I could have kids since I had DJ, and honestly, I started thinking maybe it wasn't meant to be for us. Deb found out about Tatiana, and we got into a fight. She said she couldn't take another miscarriage and would get an abortion. I didn't think that was wise, given her issues. She did it anyway, and that's when I just... checked out."

"Finally, we get to Tatiana. As you recall, we didn't cover her in our previous session," Laura reminded, as if we needed her to keep us informed. "Is Tatiana currently expecting your baby?"

He paused, then answered confidently, "Yes. She's having a girl."

My heart dropped to my stomach. *This mothafucka. Seriously?* This was the first time he actually said it. He was all stumbling over his words last time, but now he's just laying it out there. Tatiana was pregnant with a little girl. *How could this be? Was God against me? What did I do to deserve this?* I held my breath, trying so hard to keep everything from exploding out of me.

"Could you tell me more about Tatiana?" Laura looked directly at me, studying my reaction. "Debra, are you doing okay?"

Bitch, you see I'm not okay! That's what I wanted to say. I settled on, "I'm good." She could clearly see how physically uncomfortable I was with his confession. Yet, this was the work I signed up for and I was not a punk. *Bring it on, beloved.* I had to channel Iyanla Vanzant because my life needed fixing.

"Tati..."

"Don't do that! We will use her full name, no nicknames." I hissed at Derrick.

He looked annoyed, but complied. "Man, Tatiana's beautiful. I was instantly drawn to her. She's twenty-five, a bit younger than I usually go for, but I couldn't resist. She looked exotic. I saw her at the coffee and cigar bar near Deb's job, rolling cigars behind the counter. It was just... sexy. I had to find out more. I knew it was trouble, but honestly, I didn't care about the mess I was getting into. I knew the consequences and just didn't care. Home was just too much; nothing I did was ever good enough for Deb."

"I think this might be a good point to pause. Debra, could you share with us how you were feeling at that time? What was going through your mind?"

"I think, deep down, I wanted Derrick to feel the same pain I did. The miscarriages were beyond my control, but the abortion was my way of fighting back. I wanted to send him a message: change your ways, or I'll make decisions that hurt you too! I was not in my right mind. It was definitely one of the biggest mistakes in my life." I paused to take a deep breath; the session was draining. Laura didn't break her focus, she was completely locked in.

"What were you really feeling and thinking during all of this?"

"He's right, I was obsessed. I needed him close all the time. He was tied to Shayla because of DJ, and I wanted the same commitment. Family was important to both of us. We had these big dreams about our life together, where we'd live, how many kids we'd have. I was honest with him about my doubts about carrying a child. He swore he'd always be there, no matter what. And I believed him. I really did. But I've learned that promises of that magnitude are rarely, if ever, kept."

"Your wedding vows are a promise of that magnitude. Did you believe he would honor them at the time?" Laura asked.

"I trusted every word he said then. But now, I know better. It's easy to see things clearly in hindsight."

"Although you did not do your homework, Derrick, I feel as though you have answered much of what I asked of Debra. You really need to decide if you want to work on your marriage. You said you're not sure you can give her what she needs, but you definitely can't while you're still seeing Tatiana. Are you thinking about ending things with Tatiana to explore if your marriage can be restored?"

A heavy silence settled in.

CHAPTER 6

Week 2

Thursday Morning

Being in the grief-stricken hospital always gave me a chilling sense of déjà vu. The bustling people, the insistent beeping, the frantic EMTs carrying patients–it all brought me right back to that moment on the cold linoleum floor in my college bathroom. I had spent so long avoiding the trauma, the PTSD, the triggers. Denial had been my shield against the pain. But therapy was pushing me to face it, to excavate the unhealed parts of myself. I knew the life within me needed me to be whole, to be healthy and liberated from the past, to break free from the cycle of dysfunction.

"Mrs. Covington?" The nurse scanned the room, checking her clipboard.

I gradually raised my hand to let them know I was present, grabbed my purse, and followed the nurse into the doctor's office.

"How are you today?" she inquired with an almost unnervingly pleasant tone, displaying a joy that seemed out of place.

"I'm well. I'm ready to confirm what I know and what you need evidence of." I laughed quietly. The nurse, with her steady smile, directed me to the scale. *Oh snap! I gained five pounds already. And to think, I thought I was missing meals.*

"Have a seat, please, while I check your temperature and blood pressure." Her hands were icy, raising goosebumps and making my arm hair stand up.

After taking my vitals and prepping me, she ushered me into the small room. Yet again, I found myself alone in the cold, cramped hospital room. I glanced at my phone, still no word from Derrick. I'd intentionally kept this appointment to myself. I wanted to do this alone. He also didn't ask, which confirmed he didn't want to be a part. I'd hoped the pregnancy would push him one way or another, but I was still completely in the dark about his feelings.

My eyes were drawn to the images and diagrams on the walls. The one outlining the stages of the pregnancy and body transformation really struck me. It was a stark reminder of how far I had to go, still in the first trimester, navigating uncharted territory. My small embryo, like a kidney bean, depended on me to carry them to the end, unlike last time. I promised us both that I'd do better this time, not let my emotions mess things up. This time, I would embrace the progress, finding joy and serenity in the miracle growing within me, with or without the father.

"Knock, knock." Dr. Anson gave a little tap on the door, letting me know she was coming in. She seemed a lot calmer than I thought she'd be, so naturally, I got ready for some bad news.

"Hey, Debra. How are you feeling?"

"I'm a mess. Nervous, excited, scared, frustrated—all of it." I answered.

"I see," Dr. Anson noted, making entries on the computer. "Your blood pressure is slightly elevated. We'll need to check it again to determine if a follow-up appointment is necessary."

I nodded. High blood pressure was nothing new. I'd heard much worse news before. It didn't faze me any more than I'd already braced myself for.

"You're here for a pregnancy test and general check-up, correct? This isn't our first time discussing this. May I ask what's changed? We had a very thorough conversation about your previous pregnancy and the medical abortion," she said, assuming I needed reminding. "How are you feeling at the moment?"

"I know what you're getting at, Dr. Anson, and I am completely sure this time. I feel in my heart that God is giving me this last chance to be a mother. I'm going to move forward, no matter what happens with my marriage. I'm so sure this is right, and I'll do absolutely anything to make sure we are both healthy and well."

"I anticipated this visit, and that's why I ensured everything was clear to avoid infection. We successfully prevented complications, allowing you to conceive again safely. The primary concern now is your Polycystic Ovary Syndrome diagnosis, which you likely inherited from your mother. However, the test is positive. You are approximately eight weeks pregnant! Congratulations! Now, we must focus on the hard work of maintaining a healthy pregnancy, including dedication to the baby and managing stress."

Strangely, confirming the news brought me discomfort. The realization, the full acceptance of carrying a life within me, amplified my nervousness. I wasn't new to this, but something felt profoundly different. Everything inside me whispered that this was it—my moment to bring a life into being. This pregnancy was going to be different.

"Debra, let me get all the uncomfortable news out of the way." Dr. Anson took a seat on the stool and scooted in closer to me. "Due to your condition, you are at a higher risk for pregnancy complications. Some of those complications may be miscarriage, gestational diabetes, preeclampsia, high blood pressure, or preterm birth, which we will continue to monitor through your urine samples." She removed her stethoscope and placed it on my chest. "Big breath in. And out." She measured my heart rate and continued, "It does not mean that this will be your fate, but you are at a higher risk of developing any one of those." She then moved to my back and listened. "Tell me a little bit more about your mom and her health."

"As far as I know, my mom had a lot of trouble getting pregnant. She mentioned irregular periods, and I suspect she had cysts, though I can't say for certain. It didn't seem to bother her too much, or maybe she was just very good at hiding it."

"Did she have any issues with her weight?"

"Not at all. My mom is really good about staying in shape and eating healthy."

"Rest assured, we'll be here to guide you and work together to prevent or mitigate those risks. We'll set up your ultrasound appointment for approximately two weeks from today. Do you have any questions at this time?"

"I have a million questions to ask, but none that are relevant or pressing at this time."

"There's something I'm a bit concerned about..." Dr. Anson began, but she was stopped mid-sentence by the distinct and loud shouting that erupted in the hallway.

"Deb? Which room are you in?"

Hearing Derrick's voice approach, I instinctively wanted to disappear, hoping he wouldn't find me. My body went completely rigid. Dr. Anson's glance confirmed she'd observed the shift in my energy and posture.

"That's something I want to address with you when we're alone," she whispered, hearing his voice approaching and growing louder.

The door inched open, and he poked his head in. "Oh good; you're still here. I really wanted to be on time, but the traffic was crazy."

"Ah, Mr. Covington, welcome. We were just discussing important details about Debra's pregnancy and condition. I was asking if she had any questions."

"So, it's official? My baby is really pregnant."

"The results are definitive: you both will be parents. Are there any questions I can answer for you? Or anything about how you, Mr. Covington, can offer support to your wife? I have some informative pamphlets about what to do when you're expecting."

"Nah, she's good. My baby is tough! Whatever we gotta do, we will do it."

"It's crucial that she receives your support throughout this process, because it's going to be challenging. She'll require ample rest and a calm, stress-free home."

"You'd better tell that to the bad ass kids at her job. Them the ones that be stressin' her out." Derrick touted.

"Now that we're all together, I want to make sure we're on the same page. Is there a date that works best for the both of you to schedule the first ultrasound?" The question was rhetorical. She continued without waiting for a response. "Based on your last menstrual period, we estimate you're about eight weeks pregnant. We'll get a more accurate due date and confirm the number of babies at the next appointment."

"Yeah, I wanna be here for that. Debra tried to leave me out of this appointment, but it's all good. Stress-free, right babe?" He winked at me sarcastically, then gave the doctor a big smile. "We got this! I'm here and not going anywhere."

"Would you like to know the baby's gender?" Dr. Anson asked cautiously.

"Hell yeah, we want to know! I know it's a little boy in there. I can't have two girls on the way." Derrick blurted out without thinking.

His insensitivity disgusted me. "Honestly, Doctor, I just want a healthy baby and a healthy pregnancy. Whatever I am carrying,

I want them to be healthy."

"That's a perfectly normal way to feel. With your condition and circumstances, that mindset is ideal. It's incredibly important that you prioritize rest and take things slow. Follow the dietary guidelines, and things should go well. If you notice anything unusual or feel any discomfort, please don't hesitate to reach out to me. You can text my cell anytime. And of course, for any emergencies, call 911."

"Doc, I told you we are good. We ain't gonna need none of that. This ain't my first rodeo. Whatever she needs, I can take care of it." Derrick said, becoming more assertive.

"While I appreciate your confidence, Mr. Covington, I am obligated, as her physician, to thoroughly explain all the details." Turning to me, she asked, "Debra, are you fully understanding everything I'm telling you?"

"I can't help it, but I feel you're trying to get at something here."

"Derrick, stop! You're doing too much! She's talking to me. You're not even supposed to be here!" I insisted.

"What? This is my baby, too! You trippin.' Y'all females always trippin.' All up in a nigga face, gimme this, I need that. Then when you get pregnant, all of a sudden you start gettin' amnesia' and forget your common sense. Then you'll be mad if I ain't here and around. You want me to be *that* nigga, so you can go yappin' to yo homegirls about how I ain't shit?"

"Didn't nobody say all that, Derrick. Let Dr. Anson do her job and don't bring our home life into it."

"Mr. Covington, could you please step out for a moment? I need to speak with your wife privately," Dr. Anson requested politely, watching my reaction.

"Hell nah! I'm not stepping outside. Whatever you need to speak with her about, you can say while I am present. Me stepping out is a set-up for you to ask some bullshit-ass-questions. I ain't stupid!" He clenched his fists, trying to stay calm. I could practically feel the tension radiating off him.

"Dr. Anson, it's all good. We are fine and I'm comfortable with him being in the room." I insisted.

While Derrick's attention was elsewhere, Dr. Anson scribbled a note and discreetly passed it to me. I understood the unspoken message. I slipped it into my purse for safekeeping.

"The baby is developing rapidly at this stage, and is currently around the size of a raspberry, We're seeing the early stages of arm and foot development. We also need to cover your prenatal care and map out the next 30 weeks. I'm here to support you..." she hesitated, looking at Derrick, "...both of you, throughout this entire process. Are you currently on any medications or supplements?"

"No."

"Derrick, since you're here, this is a good time to ask about any genetic birth defects in your family history."

"Not that I know of," he responded, a bit confused about her question.

"What about cardiac defects or learning disabilities?"

"What type of question is that? What the hell is a cardiac defect? And ain't no special people in my family."

"Derrick, don't be ignorant." I retorted.

"It's no problem, Debra. I am here to educate." Dr. Anson stated reassuringly.

"And why are you not asking Debra all these questions? You think I am going to contaminate the baby or something?"

"Debra completed a pre-appointment survey, and she answered 'unknown' to some questions about your family history. Now that you're here, I'd like to ask you directly to ensure her chart is accurate." Dr. Anson made some notes on the computer. "Regarding your question, cardiac defects are congenital issues that affect the heart's structure and how it functions, including blood circulation. Your lack of knowledge about it suggests it's probably not a factor in your immediate family. As research on the causes is ongoing, we always begin with genetic factors."

"My fault, Doc. I didn't know that. Thank you for breaking that down," Derrick responded calmly.

"Of course. I want to make sure you both understand each step of this process. Next, we'll need to do a breast and pelvic exam to check the size of your uterus and the shape of your pelvis. You recently had a Pap smear, so we won't need to repeat that today. Before you go, please stop by the lab for some blood tests, including an STI screening. It's important to do this because any STDs can affect the baby and need to be treated right away."

CHAPTER 7

Week 2

Friday Night

"Girrrl. Yo' husband came into the shop today acting up!" Tanya shouted as soon as I picked up the phone.

"Hey... and Good Evening to you too!"

"Can you talk?" she whispered. "Did Derrick come back home yet?"

"Yes, I can talk and Derrick ain't home. It's Friday night; he probably went out to the bar with his boys. You were at the shop today, I assume?" I asked rhetorically.

"You damn right I was at the shop! Pete asked me to come in and braid a few of his clients. It was slow at *my* shop, so I helped him out and guess who came strolling in, running his mouth?" At this point, she returned to full volume.

"Who?" I asked, to add to the suspense she was creating. Even though she clearly revealed who it was.

"Yo' damn husband! He came in with a chip on his shoulder. As soon as I heard 'Debra' roll off his lips, it locked me in. See, Pete doesn't know we know each other, so he just lets him talk. And

I was not the only one all-ears, because some fine-ass-chocolate-young-man took an issue with some of the stuff he was saying. He didn't like the fact that Derrick had too many negative things to say about you and stepped to him."

The Black barbershop has always been a safe-haven for Black men all over the world. So, when Derrick tells me he is going to the barbershop, I know he is going to get away from *me*. He can cut his own hair and is very cheap about paying someone else to do what he knows and likes to do himself. But I don't take it personally because I too need space from him *and* Tanya is co-manager of the shop with her fiancé, Pete. She spends most of her free time there when she is not at *RQ Hair Care Salon*. She dishes all the tea back to me when he comes in running his mouth. Even though I get the scoop, I rarely use it against him, but this time was different. Tanya called me in an uproar, not allowing me a chance to answer any of her investigative questions; let me know exactly what time it was.

"Wait, wait, wait! Back up a second. I need all the juicy details. Who is this chocolate-fine-man you speak of?" I asked, being messy.

"Girrrl. I think his name was Jamel. He's new to the shop, but he low-key broke man-code, and may not be allowed back."

I was completely speechless, struggling to find my words. I could barely continue the conversation with her. "You gotta slow down and tell me everything." I insisted, finally getting my words out. After that, I didn't say another word except for an occasional "what?", "no!", "stop playing", "you're lyin'", but other than that I stayed tuned in what felt like a live podcast episode of *Tanya's Barbershop Tea*.

Her retelling of the story went something like this:

"Pete, this bitch is driving me crazy. I'm trying not to be done, but I can't do this shit no more."

"My man, it can't be that bad. You and yo' girl been rockin' for five years strong. Five long ass years, dealing with yo' pussy-hoppin'-ass. Y'all are couples' goals and 'Black Love' in these streets." Pete stated sarcastically, draping the barber cape around him and prepping his clippers.

"Everybody, listen up. We are about to get into a session." One of the other barbers announced, giving anyone in earshot permission to chime in if they had any advice for him.

"Check this. Y'all know I got all the love in the world for Deb. I talk about her all the time, but love ain't doing it no more. It ain't enough. This bitch is drivin' me crazy."

"Sounds like you don' got in Tatiana's drawls again." Pete chuckled, not worried about how messy he was being.

"It's not even that. My wife doesn't do it for me anymore. All she does is get on my damn nerves. Complaining about this and that. She always got the head wrap on her head, covered from head-to-toe. That shit turns me off, especially when I got Tati sending me naked pics throughout the day. I get home and I'm trying to find an excuse to get out of that bitch. We ain't fucking and we ain't sleeping in the same bed. I'm in the guest bedroom. What the hell am I supposed to do? I'm still a man. It's almost like no competition with this other woman. She makes it so easy."

"Bruh, you think the grass is greener, don't you?" Pete asked.

"I don't think it's greener. I *know* it is greener! I love my wife and it *still* ain't enough. I don't want to be at home. To get her off my back, I pick fights with the bitch. *And* this woman got us into counseling. Why the fuck would I want to tell some old White bitch our problems?"

"My man, you might want to keep your voice down. We don't all want to hear your bitch-ass sob story."

"This is when Jamel walked in." Tanya narrated, breaking character to make sure I was following the dialogue. "He must have heard right before he mentioned your name. He came, clued in and curious. Jamel sat right down in the waiting chairs by the window and nodded to Shawn to let him know he had arrived. Shawn gave him a sign to let him know he would get to him in ten minutes."

"My guy, who *is* you?" Derrick questioned.

"I'm the mothafucka that asked you to keep your voice down." Jamel sat back, unfazed with the confidence that Derrick would stay in his place.

"You don't look like you're from around here, so I suggest you mind your own business."

"I heard you mention Debra Tucker, so I made it my business."

"The fuck you mean Debra Tucker? You mean my wife, Debra Covington?"

"Oh, so now she's your wife? I thought she was a *bitch* a

minute ago?"

"Are you fucking wit' my wife?" Derrick questioned, perking up in his chair.

"I don't think that's your concern, since you seem to be done with her. And no, I'm not fucking her. I fucked her–past tense! And it sounds like I need to hit her up again, cause yo goofy ass ain't handling business."

"Girlllll… the whole barbershop got silent and waited in suspense to see what Derrick was gonna do. He, of course, did nothing. He brushed him off and didn't say nothin' else."

"What?" I could not believe what I was hearing. Jamel took up for me. Why would he do that? How did he even know Derrick was talking about me?

"Yes, girl. He was about to tear the club up fo' yo' ass. Is there something you ain't told me? You holding out on the tea? Ain't no man just starting shit in the barbershop for no reason."

Tanya was missing out on a lot of gossip, but me having an affair with Jamel wasn't part of it. Though, I admit, I wished it was. Then I would have some much-needed excitement and satisfaction.

"No, girl. We are not having sex, if that is what you're asking. I ran into his fine ass the other day at the B.A.R.T station. He was my first."

"Yo' first? As in, the one who popped the cherry?"

"Yes, girl. Back in the day when we were young and dumb.

And I got pregnant."

"You're lyin.' On the first time?"

"On the first time. I couldn't believe it either. If I didn't have that miscarriage back in college, my whole life would be different."

"He let you go away to college knowing you were preggo?"

"He didn't know. He still doesn't know."

"I don't care how much you try to downplay it, ain't no man huffin' and puffin' in the barbershop off some young, back-in-the-day, little girl coochie!"

"Well, I guess *he* did. I'm not surprised Derrick didn't do anything," I said, trying my best to change the subject. "Derrick is non-confrontational with other men. He is the definition of a bitch-ass. Excuse my expression, but he is. He wouldn't have a problem getting in my face, but if he knows he could get his ass whooped, he will not press the issue."

"Pete wouldn't have let nothing go down in his shop, anyway. Derrick is his boy, so he would have broke it up, if necessary. My man doesn't play them games in his place of business. He doesn't like nobody fucking with his money. The smoke cleared quickly, and everything went back to normal." She paused for a moment, hoping I would reconsider and come clean. "So, you're really not gonna tell me the truth? Ain't no way Deb, this man is confronting your husband on a childhood crush."

"So, you won't believe this?" I asked, changing the subject.

"What's that? Spit it out, chick!"

"I'm pregnant."

"You're lyin'. Since when? Why am I just now hearing about this?"

"The doctor confirmed it yesterday. Eight weeks."

"Oh my God Girl! Congratulations. I'm so happy for you. I know this is what you wanted." Tanya said excitedly.

"Yeah," I replied. Something in my tone must have shifted, because Tanya immediately asked her next question.

"Oh no! Is everything okay? I know I just went in and didn't even check-in with you."

"There's just a lot happening right now. And you just told me my husband is in the shop talking bad about me."

"I know, girl. Derrick ain't shit. But also, you ain't slick. You didn't answer my question about Jamel."

"If there's something to tell, you will be the first to know. But I gotta go. He is calling me now."

"Who's calling you? Derrick or Jamel? Debra?...Debra!"

Click.

CHAPTER 8

Week 3

Wednesday Early Evening

I was at the end of my rope. My body, mind, and heart were all pulling me in different directions, leaving me utterly depleted and unwilling to play Derrick's games. The universe had to give me something, *anything*. I desperately needed a reason to stay in this loveless marriage. Let's be real; the only thing that got me out of bed and here today was the fact that these sessions were free. I knew I wouldn't get another chance at free counseling.

We arrived separately, practically dodging each other in the parking lot as we pulled up almost at the same moment. It was as if we'd both tried to time our arrival to miss the other, only to fail miserably. He brushed past me without a word, letting himself into the building. I took a deep breath, trying to brace myself. Things hadn't changed, and I was devoid of hope. My secret wish was that he'd get fed up and walk out of the session, leaving me to work on myself. We checked in with the receptionist.

"I don't want to be here." Derrick mumbled under his breath, observably agitated and ready to go. For once we were in alignment—I did not want to be here either.

"Go ahead. Leave. Do what you do best and just walk out." My response was now louder, more audible, and targeted at him. I sat down.

Derrick sat down across from me. "Baby, don't play with me right now. I told yo' ass I would be here, I would show up, and I am. This is some bullshit, but I'm a man of my word."

"Since when?" I pushed, enacting part one of the plan.

"Since I told yo'..."

"Mrs. Schatz will see you now." The receptionist gladly interrupted what she felt might be an unpleasant situation about to pop off in the lobby. The normal chick had the day off. Lucky for her because I had some choice words for her too.

Derrick was up and moving before I could even register it, his eyes fixed anywhere but on me. He marched down the hall to the meeting room, leaving me to follow. He made no effort to assist me, not even a glance to check if I was alright. There was no gentle hand on my back, no offer to help me to the couch. As far as I knew, our disagreements didn't change the fact that I was pregnant.

Keeping as much space between us as I could manage, we both sat in a heavy silence, waiting for our "referee" to arrive.

Laura couldn't help but notice the wide gap between us when she arrived and took her seat. "How was your weekend? I think I'll start with you, Derrick," she said, her tone consistently pleasant.

"It was alright," Derrick kept his eyes low, and hands clasped, looking down toward the floor.

"Okay, just alright?" she asked, pushing a little. "I want to remind you that this is a safe space, and it's a chance to address everything that's been going on between you since our last session."

"I'm not even gonna lie. I'm struggling with this therapy shit. I'm struggling to see the point. You asked me in the last session if I was ready to stop seeing Tatiana. And I thought about it. I mean, I thought long and hard and weighed my options. Then, I go to the barbershop the other day, and ran into some nigga that she is fuckin' with." Laura cleared her throat. "My bad. My apologies, that she is messin' with, and I'm trying to figure out why I would stop what I'm doing, and she's doing the same?"

He was on a roll. Like, come up for air, baby! I could see him physically becoming more and more agitated as every word rolled off of his lips.

"And get this, she had a doctor's appointment and tried to stop me from going. Like that's not *my* baby. She can't keep me from my child. That's why females end up alone." He sighed heavily and adjusted his position.

"I appreciate your honesty, Derrick, regarding your feelings and the events of the last week. It's crucial to remember that this process is effective only when both of you are committed to the outcome, whatever that may be." She paused thoughtfully, then added, "Debra, could you share about your week and maybe provide some more context to Derrick's statements?"

I sat up, adjusting my posture, and took a long, dramatic pause, hoping to fuel his anger. "He's right," I stated. "I didn't want him at the appointment. And I'm still not sure about keeping the baby." I knew it was a lie, but I wanted to agitate him more.

"And what about this man that Derrick mentioned?" Laura questioned. I immediately felt she was crossing a line. I think she was being a bit messy.

"I can't confirm nor deny his allegations."

"Stop playin'. Why the hell am I here, then? Fuck this! I'm done!" He got to his feet, his eyes locking directly with mine, and he paused, expecting me to respond.

"You can sit-up-in-here and share about every woman you ran thru, but I have one indiscretion and you're done?" I questioned, keeping my voice steady.

"Debra, yo' ass is playin'. You're trying to play a man's game. You don't have a clue! You got a man that loves you."

"Do you? You have a really funny way of showing it."

"I come home to yo' ass every night. You think them other..." he hesitated. You could see him reworking his words in his mind to not disrespect me in front of Laura. "You think them other females don't want me to come home to *them*? They feel some type of way and let me know it, but I come home to yo' ass."

Clap, clap, clap. I stood up, giving him a standing ovation. "Thank you, baby, for coming home to your wife like you're supposed to do. You should receive the *Husband of the Year* award for your commitment to marital excellence."

"Fuck it! I'm out!" He stormed out of the room and didn't look back.

"Oh, he's big mad." I chuckled to myself. "Go!"

I slumped back onto the couch, gripping the armrest. A wave of unusual exhaustion had washed over me the past few days. I looked at Laura, and she was just staring at me, like she was either shocked or let down. I couldn't be sure, and I didn't particularly care, as she hadn't yet spoken, and her expressions seemed to run together.

"Debra, do you want to continue?" she asked, breaking the silence politely.

"I don't know. Should I? Derrick is gone. What's the point?"

"The sessions are covered, so let's use the remaining 35 minutes. My focus is on both of you, and we can dedicate this time to talking about you."

I nodded my head. "I would like that."

"Let's set aside the marriage stuff for a moment. What else is going on with you personally?"

"Well, my brother is about to be released from prison next week."

"And how are you feeling about that?"

I paused, took a deep breath, and continued, "Inside, I'm numb and terrified. The pregnancy, the broken marriage, my brother's release—it's all blurring together. I don't know which way is up."

"What you could be feeling is emotional numbness." Noticing my puzzled expression, she continued, "Emotional numbness is usually an unconscious defense mechanism against painful emotions, whether it's anxiety, stress, or even trauma. Any kind of trauma can trigger a stress response that overwhelms you and leads to this state of collapse, including emotional numbness. To combat it, we can use talk therapy, among other methods. We could also try some grounding exercises if you're open to it."

"I'm okay with talking for now." Therapy was already a stretch at this point. Grounding with her would be entirely too awkward.

"Wonderful. Let's continue then." She picked up her notepad and waited for me to begin.

"I'm the baby of the family, but expected to always have it together. Samson got to be the fuck up, I'm sorry, the *mess up* and I had to know better and do better. I got good grades and tried my best to follow the rules and he still got all the attention and all the love and praise."

"I'm curious; what were you expecting?" she inquired.

"I was expecting for them to pour into *me* and *see me*. It felt like my mom just hated me, and I hadn't done anything to deserve it. Samson, who caused so much friction, was always her angel, no matter what."

"Let's revisit what you said about your mother. I want to explore that further. What's your sense of what your mom thinks about you? How do you believe she perceives you?"

"Now that I'm older and lived a bit, I think she saw me as herself. I think she felt I would end up like her. That I had it too easy and was ungrateful."

"Is that true? Are you ungrateful?"

"Not at all! I think she felt she needed to be hard on me, so I would not be gullible in the world. That I would not fall for anything or let anyone take advantage of me. Black girls are getting kidnapped left and right in the streets. She knew what Oakland was like for young Black girls and she wanted to keep me protected. I have a missing student and I think she may have been kidnapped for sex trafficking. My mama was trying to protect me from that. I can say all of this now, but then... it was another story." I felt some relief once I finished speaking.

"I understand, and I want to emphasize that you know you're not ungrateful. Your thoughts and opinions are what guide you. The more you release those negative thoughts and hold onto the positive ones, the better you'll feel. Remember, mental wellness is something you have to work at, and it takes time." She gave me a steady look, gauging my understanding. It was all starting to make sense. "Alright, let's get back to Samson and his release now."

The reality was setting in. "He will be out next Friday! My brother will be free. Samson was always ambitious and wanted more for himself. He didn't want anyone to do it for him because he thought he could get it himself. But he just couldn't stay out of them–damn streets! All I wanted for him was to be content. Not another statistic. So many Black men have been shot and killed, and he wanted to buy guns and run around like he was a thug. How could he protect me if he was out there?"

"Did he protect you?"

"He did until he got out of hand. When I was leaving to go to college, he was angry. He didn't want to listen to anyone...

and... when I found out he had purchased a gun... I... I knew I had lost him. He wasn't the same."

"What do you feel changed?"

"We might have felt similar. He got all the attention but wanted space, while I felt unloved and neglected. I dealt with it by focusing on school and work. And since Samson was out in the streets, I really didn't have anyone looking out for me or keeping track of me."

"I'm wondering what shifted. Did it bother you that Samson couldn't fill the parental role you might have hoped for?"

"I'd never looked at it from that angle. I simply wanted him present. He was the golden-child, regardless of his behavior. I grew resentful and envious. Everything revolved around Samson. When I left for college, my parents made it a quick trip so they could rush back and worry about him, not me. And what happened? He had someone over and got himself kicked out. All while I was unknowingly pregnant." I cut myself off, feeling like I was going on and on.

"You're doing perfectly fine. Keep going." Laura insisted.

"I lied to my friends, saying it was my first time that I was a virgin. But I wasn't. I felt ashamed, despite knowing everyone else was sexually active. I didn't want to shatter their image of me as the 'good girl,' an image I'd started to believe myself. I saw things in black and white: Samson was bad, I was good. It was that clear to me." I reached for a tissue, tears welling up. "I'd convinced myself that I was the only one without flaws. That's when the lies began, when I started creating this alter ego."

"'Alter ego?'" Laura queried, making a notation. "Please provide further details regarding this alter ego. Does he or she possess a name or designation?"

"*She* doesn't have a name. It's more like a feeling, a state-of-mind. There was this presence residing within me, and I possessed the ability to consciously activate it. She made life more vibrant and expressive. *She* became my protector."

"So, do you think you were feeling pretty good about yourself back then?"

"No. Things were really bad, but I pretended I was fine. I lied to protect myself and others. Before college, I slept with Michael, Samson's best friend. We agreed to keep it a secret because Samson would have gone ballistic."

"I know this might be a difficult question, but is there any chance that the father of the baby you lost could have been his friend, or someone else?"

"Honestly, I don't really know. But I'm content with believing it was Jamel's."

"What is your understanding of the reasons behind Samson's disapproval of your dating his friend?"

"Probably because he wasn't a good person. He knew his friend was just as triflin' as he was. But I didn't care. I just wanted to piss him off, see if he'd notice. I even tried to get caught... But he was too wrapped up in his own stuff to even see what was going on."

"But nobody noticed, did they?"

"Right." I wasn't sure where else this conversation could lead. It felt like we'd reached a dead end, a point beyond which I couldn't see.

Shifting gears, Laura asked, "How frequently does your alter ego show up now? Is *she* still with you?"

"Absolutely! *She* is here now, or she was earlier."

"In your view, what could she be protecting you from now?"

For a moment, I considered the question. It felt subtly deceptive, and I chose not to offer a reply.

"I want to be clear: I don't think you're crazy, and I don't believe you have a severe mental illness. I see this alternative personality as a protective strategy, something you use when you feel afraid or isolated. Our time is nearly up, and I want to provide you with some resources for support." She gave me a pamphlet for a support group and chatline. I took it with some hesitation. "Pretty Heart Inc. offers a wonderful parenting support group and a specialized group for pregnant women who have experienced trauma. Connecting with other women can help you feel less alone."

I nodded gently. "Thank you."

"If you experience any heaviness, anxiety, or distress concerning the reunion with your brother, please reach out to this number immediately. Someone is available 24 hours a day, 7 days a week."

CHAPTER 9

Week 4
Sunday Late Morning

"Edmond, my love, do you have the final list of everything we need from the store?"

"Yes, dear."

"I need you to get out early tomorrow to get everything, so I'm not waiting around all day. I need all-week to prep for the party." Charlene moved methodically between the living room and kitchen, gathering items and placing them in a meticulously arranged pile.

"Honey, I'm not going to let this stress me. You can worry all you want, but I'm staying relaxed. I know what I need to do. It'll all be fine." Edmond positioned himself with his remote in his favorite recliner. He was on his last ounce of patience with Charlene. She had a few more requests before he started tuning her out.

"I still haven't heard from everyone who I invited. I just don't want to run out of food and drinks if more people come than RSVP'd."

"Now you know our people don't RSVP anymore. They just show up. And the long ass list of items you have for me to get, I would be shocked if we run out of anything. You got me buying up the whole store like we're doing a spoon feed for the neighborhood."

Ignoring any potential answers from him, Charlene continued her monologue, "I talked to Lydia, and she's going to stop by. She's bringing her famous fried chicken, baked macaroni and cheese, and her okra medley."

"You got folks bringing food, too?" Edmond said, shaking his head in disbelief, and switched to CNN. He'd been obsessing over world news and political scandals ever since all the mess with Samson and Calvin.

"Honey, I know but, everyone wants to help out and bring something, so I didn't fuss with her about it." She rummaged through the closet, looking for more items to add to the pile of party supplies. "Babe, do you know what time Debra is stopping by? Did she text you back? And have you seen my glass punch bowl? I know I placed it in this closet after the last gathering." She removed a few more items from the closet.

"She said she'd be here soon. I texted her an hour ago, and she said she was on her way. And you know I avoid that closet to avoid your nagging," he smirked.

"Good. I could really use her help, going through these old boxes of his stuff. I want to set up his room with some of the things that meant a lot to him before he went in."

"You ladies handle that project. I'm not getting involved. Don't ask. I'll get the store stuff, but then I'm clocking out."

"Oh honey, look what I found." She held up an old photo of Samson when he was a toddler, covered in lotion while fully clothed. "He looked so innocent then, that sweet little face. But he knew he was about to tear his ass up for getting into my brand new *Neutrogena* with his clothes on."

"You let that boy get away with murder." Edmond stopped, regretting his choice of words. "Sorry, I shouldn't have said that. You let him do whatever he wanted. I knew then he was not cut from the same cloth as I was."

Charlene paused, sensing the shift in the atmosphere. Tears welled in her eyes. They usually avoided the topic of Samson not being Edmond's son, a truth that had deeply affected the Tucker family. Despite everything Samson had done, that revelation was hard to accept. Edmond had always had his suspicions, but never voiced them to Charlene. He knew he'd hurt her enough already and couldn't bear to add to her pain.

"Honey, I know this is difficult for you, too. I would have taken it to the grave. No one could have convinced me that he was not your son, especially after all we went through." Charlene walked over and sat beside him on the edge of the couch. "I prayed with all my might that he was yours, but in my heart, I knew otherwise. God wasn't going to do me any favors."

"And to think, I only learned the truth because he killed his father. What a twisted life. I blame myself too. I didn't accept him. He was always too soft, trying to be something that he wasn't…

or what I thought he wasn't. I wanted him to be more like me, but he kept going back to the streets. I warned him he'd get in trouble, but he wouldn't listen. My mistakes were not enough for him—he had to make his own." Edmond shifted uncomfortably, fighting back his emotions. Charlene understood and moved back to the closet to create distance and distract herself.

"You were the same way. You always wanted to figure things out on your own and wouldn't listen to anyone. I recall numerous instances where you outright disobeyed your father," Charlene reminded him.

"You damn right! That man couldn't tell me nothing! He wasn't in my life. He just wanted to pretend he was doing something. Whatever he said, I did the opposite, so no one could say I was like him. I was my own man."

"And that's not Samson? You're more alike than you think. But that doesn't change the fact that you've been his father since day one. Why would you let a DNA test erase that? Every lesson, every sport, every bit of guidance came from you. No other man has shaped him the way you have."

Edmond stood up and went to Charlene by the closet. He took her hand. "It shouldn't bother me, but it does. When I look at his face, I see Calvin, and then I see him making love to you, and it makes me sick. How could I have been so stupid, so blind, to let you get so desperate that you'd go to Calvin Rogers? He could laugh in my face, and he'd be right. He had both of my ladies. And both of you lied about me being a father. Debra's all I got."

"Do you hear yourself? Calvin didn't have me. We had a

meaningless moment together… or a few meaningless moments."

"I don't want to hear all that."

"You thought I wanted to hear about you and Raquel; and the kid you were always taking care of?"

"You knew I was with her, and you came knocking anyway."

"You made it seem like y'all were over."

"Look, you knew I wasn't ready to settle down then. You met me when I was fresh in the game. I was too handsome to be with one woman. Y'all wouldn't let me." He flexed his muscles and puffed out his chest.

Charlene playfully smacked him upside his head. "Wake up! Stop dreaming. I knew what I wanted, and I went after it and here we are now. A lot of drama, pain, and chaos later, but here we are. I'm sure God used Samson to straighten us out." They locked eyes and broke out in a deep belly laugh.

***

I knew my mother would be stressed with Samson's release just a week away, so I took my time driving over there. My strategy was to arrive after she'd already exhausted herself with my daddy, and not have much left for me to do. I aimed for a quick thirty-minute visit, in-and-out, maybe stretch it to an hour if I was lucky, and then bail.

Since I was early, I went to Rolling Hills Memorial Park. The discussions surrounding Samson's homecoming had triggered an urgent need for release. I had to make my peace with it, keep any bad juju away from my baby. I wished we could just be a normal family, even though we were so far from it. We presented a facade of ordinary life to the world, a deliberate effort to maintain privacy, to keep people out of our business. Our social media was a carefully constructed narrative. I refrained from sharing my personal life on Instagram, choosing instead to dedicate the majority of my posts to positive affirmations.

It was nice to see the cemetery so quiet, without many visitors. The atmosphere was indeed its typical solemn peace. The sight of flowers and teddy bears scattered across numerous graves served as a poignant reminder of the many young Black men whose lives had been cut short by violence. My visit wasn't any different. It seemed strange that I was often drawn to Calvin's grave, given our history. He was buried in the fancy Lotus Garden Estates, with that beautiful view of the bay, and it had become my only escape. I needed to unravel the mystery of Samson, why he was so different from me, so I came to talk to his father about it. I just needed to unload all the mess in my life.

"Umm... Hi Calvin. It's me... again." The conversations I had felt incredibly real, to the point where I was thinking of him almost as a stepfather. I didn't need another father, but he was Samson's father, so we were connected somehow.

"So, Samson's getting out soon. I doubt you care, 'cause he's why we're here in the first place. But we both know it's not all your fault." I checked to see if I was still alone. I thought about crouching down on the grass, but a strange, unsettling feeling that I might inherit that bad juju, stopped me. Instead, I found a seat on the bench.

My phone buzzed. It was a text from Derrick. I glanced at it but didn't open it, wanting to avoid the "read" receipt. I didn't want him to know I was ignoring him.

"You're probably gonna be surprised by this, but I'm not exactly thrilled about Samson coming home. I got used to him being locked up." I looked over my shoulder and around the cemetery. "To be real with you, I felt safer with him in there, even though he always had my back. The streets messed him up. I could see it in his eyes. They took my brother from me. The day after he was held at gunpoint, just before his 18th birthday, he decided he belonged to the streets. He had to 'go hard' and 'secure the bag' and 'let niggas know what was up'." I made air quotes as I recalled his words; they sounded ridiculous now. "I was terrified Samson would become like you, turn against our father, and tear our family apart. I had to protect us. I had to report him for killing Tony Watkins. I couldn't trust anyone; our parents had lied. They wouldn't do what was needed, so I did. Now he's coming home, and I don't even know if he knows. What if he tries to kill me? He ruined everything! You ruined everything!" I cried out.

"Is that little Debra Tucker?" *Who is it this time?* The Bay Area felt smaller every day. The voice was just a few feet away. I instinctively closed my jacket to conceal my baby bump and forced myself to appear composed.

"Oh, my God! Charles! I can't believe it. What are you doing here?" He hadn't changed a bit, as if time had frozen.

"Nah, nah, you gotta show me some love first." He wrapped his arms around me, lifting me up briefly before putting me back on my feet. "Man, it's been forever since I've seen you. I talk to your pops every so often. But damn, you're all grown up now." He inspected me with a broad grin.

"Damn right I'm grown! So, what are you doin' here?" I asked again, figuring he missed it before.

"I'm up here every week, just trying to clear my head. You know Elijah's grave is just down the way in the flat memorials. I pay my respects, then I sit and stare at Calvin's grave, trying to understand it all." The initial light in his eyes faded, replaced by a stoic, almost weary look.

"Oh, that's right! Duh. I'm so sorry. I should've known that." I instantly regretted opening my mouth.

"Nah, it's cool. It's good to see a familiar face. I try to stay out of the way. It all became too much for me; I needed to distance myself. I'm just focused on work and keeping my head on straight."

"I understand." I replied, attempting to maintain control. "By the way, I saw your mother the other day; she's still doing my hair." I pointed to my head. I knew they weren't talking much and was hoping to get some juicy details.

"Yeah, I guess Mama's still at it. That's cool. I don't say too much to her. I text every now-and-then to let her know I'm alive, but I don't have nothin' else to say to her."

"That's your mama. You gotta talk to her. She did mention that she misses you."

"Nah, I'm good. I'm a grown-ass man, and she lied to me knowing how tight we were. I'm fine. She can do her thing, and I'll do mine."

"Um, so... Samson is getting released soon, did you hear?" I was hoping to fill the silence to keep him from asking me anything I wasn't ready to answer.

"Yeah, I heard that. Y'all ready for that? While some are celebrating, others might want him dead." He shook his head, clearly concerned.

"That's what my dad says. He said we have to be a unit and make sure he is protected when he comes out." I wanted to ask which side he was on, but I think I already knew.

"Your dad's a good man, and he knows what he's talking about. He lied, but I understand why. My mother, though, had no excuse. She was my rock. She knew everything about my struggles. I was in the streets, so I know what's out there. And that's why I got out of 'em. I want to live a meaningful life, leave behind a legacy."

"Do you have any kids or a special lady?"

"Yeah, I got a daughter, she's eleven. Me and her mom, we split. Didn't work out, especially since she hooked up with my boy." He looked down, kinda shuffled his hands, and said, "But I got someone special now. She knows all my shit, and we're good. I'm thinking about settling down and giving her my last name."

"Not Charles, the *Playa from the Himalayas,* Simmons. Settle down? No way!"

"Yeah, I'm for real. I'm getting old, man. I told you, I'm grown. I wanna be that dad, sitting on the porch, watching my kids play in the street. I can't wait around forever. I regret not being more present for you and Samson growing up. I missed out on all that. I even feel guilty about how he got caught up with Calvin."

"I understand. It's not your fault, and you couldn't have changed Samson's choices." It dawned on me that Samson, being Calvin's son, officially made them blood brothers. I hesitated, recalling the planned celebration. "You should come over for Samson's homecoming on Saturday. He needs to see you."

"Bet. I'll be there. Here's my number; text me the details."

"Do you still talk to Lance?" I asked. "My mom said Ms. Lydia is going to come. Lance is invited too!"

"Yeah, actually, he's the one who slept with my ex. We were young and stupid. But we don't let no ho' come between us." He chuckled. "He's my brother for life. I'll send him the details when you text them to me. I'm glad I ran into you, sis. I need to get to work. It was good seeing you, and we'll talk soon."

"It's good seeing you too!"

It was an unexpected distraction, but it was needed. What were the odds? On the day I decide to visit Calvin's grave, I run into Charles Simmons. I hadn't seen him since the funeral and the day Samson was arrested. Things were becoming too coincidental. My mission was to make amends, and the universe was orchestrating everything for that atonement.

Bzzz. Bzzz. My daddy was texting me again. This time, 911.

***

"Call Debra again, Edmond. She is taking entirely too long," Charlene nagged looking at her watch.

As soon as I shut the front door, I heard Mama fussin'. "Mama, I'm here. Daddy, you don't have to blow up my phone."

"What took you so long, Debra? I almost have everything done now," she complained.

Yes! There is a God!

"We have one week, and you know I'm starting to stress myself out about having everything perfect. I need you to help me sort through some boxes to pick out Samson's favorite things to put in his room."

"You do realize Samson is not twelve, right?" I gave her the most serious look I could muster up. "He may not even want to stay here with y'all."

"Where else would he stay? It's not like he has money or a job to pay to live anywhere else?"

"Have you considered that he might have a girlfriend? Or a boyfriend that he met while in prison and can stay with them?"

"That's something I hadn't thought of, actually. I'm going to rely on my gut feeling and believe he'll stay here. He hasn't told me otherwise."

I noticed the mess my mother created by the closet and I couldn't resist snooping. There was so much stuff piled up, I almost did not want to disrupt their placement, but my curiosity wouldn't let me leave it alone. I carefully moved the box on top to not disturb the arrangement and noticed the photo of Samson when he was 18 months. It instantly gave me flashbacks.

"Mama, why did you ruin our family?"

"What did you say to me, Debra?"

"Why did you ruin our family?" I repeated myself just as firmly and clearly as I did the first time.

"What do you mean, *ruin* our family? And how exactly did I do that?"

Keeping my back to her, I continued. "You slept with Calvin and had his baby! You knew he was an evil man. You knew Daddy would be devastated, and you kept the baby anyway!"

"Who do you think you're talking to? I want to remind you that you have yet to give birth to the baby that is growing inside of you, so you would want to watch your mouth!"

I turned to her. "I'm pregnant by my husband, not some random murderer!"

"Have you lost every good sense that God gave to you? You don't get to ask me that!"

"Baby Girl, what's gotten into you?" My daddy interjected; a bit confused how we got into this heated discussion within minutes of my arrival.

Perhaps it was a subconscious plan to flee, to avoid confronting my issues. Or maybe Calvin's memory triggered something within me. Or maybe, seeing Samson as a baby and knowing how much Mama always loved him just hurt. He always knew how to steal the moment and get all the love, sympathy, and attention, even in his absence. Throughout his incarceration, every conversation, every dollar, every tear revolved around Samson, and I hated him for it!

"Debra Tucker, you listen to me. I don't have to explain to you why I make any of the choices I make. Please understand I am not proud of what I did, but I've forgiven myself and so has your father. You have not made peace with so many things that will tear you apart if you continue to let it fester. Don't you dare speak of my past and you've yet to know and meet that baby that is growing in *your* belly. I'm certain that you'll love that child with everything in you. Even if the baby turns out just like Derrick! Have you stopped for a moment to consider your indiscretions? Babbbyyy..." She turned to keep herself from either hitting me or bursting out in tears.

"Mama, I'm sorry..."

"I don't want to hear it. Nor do I need your help. I've done some things I regret in my life, but having Samson was not one of them and until you become a mother, don't judge me."

"Mama, I'm sorry." I had said too much.

Turning back to me, her eyes locked with mine. "At Elijah's funeral, I finally found inner peace. I forgave myself, your father, and Raquel. During the service, God revealed to me through the preacher that Samson would have to bear the weight of his choices and mine. And I have carried that weight every single day."

I picked up my phone and finally read the message from Derrick.

> *Hey Baby, just so you know I'm good. I'll be home soon. I got a hotel to clear my head. Don't worry, I'm not with Tatiana. Not like it matters anyway.*

I began to answer, but then stopped myself.

CHAPTER 10

Week 4
Sunday Night

The stillness of sitting in bed and staring at nothingness, I just couldn't take anymore. The loneliness was crushing, the feeling of being unwanted, unbearable. I got into my car, driven by something I couldn't resist. Next thing I knew, I was at the hotel. I walked up to the front desk, asked for his name, got his room number—312—and was at the point of no return. My heart was pounding in the elevator, but I went up to the third floor. My heart hammered in my chest as the elevator doors opened. I slowly exited to the right, towards his room. I took another deep breath as I lifted my slightly trembling hand and knocked gently. As he opened the door, we simply stood there, our eyes searching for something unspoken. For someone to intervene and stop us from going backwards. He stepped to the side, behind the door, and opened it wider for me to walk inside. As I crossed the threshold into the dimly lit hotel room, a sense of nostalgia washed over me. The air was charged with memories that lingered from a fragrance of another time. The soft glow of the lamp on the nightstand cast gentle shadows on the walls, creating an intimate atmosphere that drew me in. His eyes devoured every inch of my body. His hand gently brushed along my waistline, motioning for me to come closer. I moved further in, my gaze meeting the bed before turning to him at the window, the moonlight sculpting his bare chest. We locked eyes, and in that moment, I saw a complex dance of longing and hesitation. It felt like a distant memory, though it was only days since we'd shared this space. We were on separate roads, and I wasn't sure if we could find our way back.

Yet, in that moment, we were reunited, our hearts beating in time with a love that had endured. The moment felt delicate. As he approached me, I felt a rush of warmth spreading through my veins, igniting a long-dormant flame within my soul. He touched me gently at first, like he was afraid I'd disappear. When our lips met, the pain melted away, and we were simply us. At that moment, I closed my eyes, losing myself in the sensation of his hands on my skin roaming my body, tracing the curves that he knew so well. Every caress of the tongue, every whispered word, every kiss, felt like a rediscovery, a rekindling of a passion that had never truly died. I found myself naked on the bed, not just physically bare, but emotionally vulnerable. My heart and soul were laid bare before him, and he gazed upon me with a hungry desire.

As our bodies became entwined, I found myself haunted again by a sense of déjà vu. It was as if I was pulled back into a past moment, a memory so vivid it felt almost real. And then, in the heat of our lovemaking, I realized the truth. It wasn't him I was making love to, not really. It was the man who had always had my heart, who at one time, had loved me through thick and thin. When our eyes connected, I acknowledged the enduring place of the past, yet knew the present held the greater weight. It was a risk, potentially a setback, but I felt no regret. Surrendering to the consuming passion, I knew I was where I was meant to be, in the arms of the man who remained my truest love.

CHAPTER 11

Week 4
Monday Morning

My morning sickness had mostly passed. I cautiously flipped my phone over, face down, on my desk to avoid the temptation of Jamel's incoming call. We had engaged in a few, okay several, very inappropriate late-night, and early morning text messages. I sensed he expected more. Ironically, I'd secretly wished he'd reach out, so I wouldn't feel responsible. His fine ass still had a hold on me. Despite my circumstances, I longed for the thrill of the chase, even if I was not available. I refused to be the one making the first move. When we ran into each other, my well had run dry. Things with Derrick were dead; we weren't doing anything. I was just craving any kind of attention I could get.

I know it sounds desperate, but I didn't care. He was the platter, and I was starving for attention. I left my door slightly open, hoping for Mr. Earl to come busting in, but he never came. Maybe this was a sign. The waiting was intense. I flipped my phone over once more, hoping for a message. Still nothing. *Was I playing hard to get, or was he?* I couldn't fight it anymore. I gently closed the door and redialed his number.

"I thought you would never call." He pleasantly responded.

"I've been thinking about what happened. It happened so fast, and I realized I came on stronger than I intended. I was just really in the moment, and I couldn't help it."

"Debra, you don't have to apologize. I wanted it too!" He was not going to make this easy for me.

"Why? You never even thought twice about me in all these years."

"I was way too much for you then. I didn't want to break your heart. You were better than that, and I didn't want to bring you in my shit."

"And now it's okay?" I questioned.

"No, it's not... I mean... I don't know. I know what I feel." His disposition shifted, and I felt it strongly.

"And what exactly do you feel?... Wait, don't answer that." I suddenly remembered what Tanya told me. "Why did you go to the barbershop and confront him?"

"Confront who?"

"You know exactly who I am talking about... Derrick." Even mentioning his name and hearing it roll off my lips gave me a rush.

"That wasn't my intention. I legit went to get my hair cut, and I saw him." He seemed sincere. "I heard him talking shit about you, and I had to shut it down. That nigga is foul," he insisted. I could hear the concern in his voice. He really wanted to defend my honor.

I sighed heavily. "We've gone too far already. I don't know what to do." I took a breath, keeping my voice down, just in case someone was listening.

"Do what's in your heart," Jamel replied.

"What does that mean?"

"It means this shit is scary. I am married too! You make me feel a way I haven't felt in years. My wife and I are solid. I love her... but what we have is some unreal movie-type-shit."

I hesitated a moment. The feeling was definitely mutual. A heaviness sat near the pit of my stomach. I could feel the flutter in my belly. "This is crazy! We can't see each other again. It happened. I needed it. You brought life back into my body and I thank you for it, but I can't come between you and your wife. And I don't want to."

"The cold part is, you already did, and we both felt it. This ain't a game!"

"What makes you better than my husband? He cheated on me and now you have cheated on your wife."

"Damn!" He immediately got quiet. The silence was loud. He sighed loudly, "You're right. I ain't no better than him, but I wish it was just that easy to walk away. I've been thinking about you every day since I saw you at the B.A.R.T station. I'm making love to my wife, thinking about you. That ain't supposed to happen. When I touched your hand, I know you felt that shit. I can't even lie to you. I was praying you would call me. And you did. The same night." He was now breathing deeply and panting, if almost begging for me to reconsider.

"Yeah, I felt it, but so what? We can't do anything about it." I demanded.

"Why did you call me, then? Why respond to my calls and texts?"

"I don't know."

"Debra, don't play with me!"

I took a deep breath. I wasn't prepared for the feelings that flooded back, like something from my youth, but amplified. It was intense. A tingling sensation scaled up and down my legs and arms. I'd never felt this with Derrick, though I knew I loved him. Was I subconsciously playing a game, driven by past trauma? *Was he simply a rebound?* I couldn't find an answer, leaving me trapped in this dilemma.

"I need you to know something. When I moved away to go to college, I was pregnant. And..."

"You were pregnant and didn't tell me?" he exclaimed, cutting me off mid-sentence.

"I had no way of contacting you." I pleaded.

"You could have reached me through Estelle, sweetheart. I wouldn't have left you alone."

"I didn't know. I was afraid, and by the time I did find out, it was too late. I'd lost the baby." My eyes filled with tears, and I reached down to gently cradle my stomach.

"Damn it, Debra. I wish you'd told me. I would have been

there for you. All these years, you never once thought to find me and let me know?"

I dabbed at my tears with a tissue, adding it to the growing pile. My papers were wet, my eyes swollen, and I felt broken. I continued, "Truthfully, I wished I could just erase it all, bury it so I wouldn't have to face it or you. If only I knew then what I know now…"

Knock. Knock. "Mrs. Covington, you have a student waiting to see you."

I muted the phone so I could respond without totally disrupting the flow of the conversation. My office wasn't ideal for this conversation, but it was the only place I could speak privately without worrying about Derrick. I felt like I was being all sneaky, which was weird. Our marriage was basically over, but I still felt guilty, like it was all my fault. I promised Mrs. Schatz that I'd work on the marriage, but I was deceiving everyone, including myself. I was lying to myself and everyone else in between.

"Mrs. Reem, please let them know I'll meet with them during 6th period. Write them a pass and send them back to class."

"Hello? Jamel?" He'd already hung up. I stared at the phone, a wave of confusion washing over me, then a text alert pulled me back.

> Jamel - I had to hop off. Wifey walked in. Meet me at the BART station at 4 PM, where we first met. We need to talk. If this is goodbye, I want to see you one last time in person.

I watched each minute tick by on the clock, time dragging. I kept wondering if he'd actually come, but I was already there, waiting. In my mind, we were escaping, and the baby was his, not my husband's. He called me "wife." Life was good. We were happy. But it was just a dream, and I knew it.

***

It was 3:44 P.M., and I was early. Every parking spot was taken. After circling the lot a few times, I parked at a nearby market. The walk would help calm my nerves. There was no reason to make a dramatic entrance. We both needed to slip back into our lives unnoticed. We'd crossed a line; nothing would be the same. We had gone too far. Our souls were connected.

I bypassed several benches soiled with graffiti, bird poop, and unrecognizable soot; and found an empty spot near the ticket machines. I fumbled around in my purse for my compact. If you stay ready, you don't have to get ready. My reflection confirmed my confidence. I heard a few men off in the distance whistling, but I ignored them. *I looked good.* A slight dryness in my mouth led me to my last peppermint, a small comfort. The station was a blur of movement; it was the best location to be inconspicuous. The glowing advertisement helped slow my racing heart. My fairytale floated before me, but the way to it remained unclear.

The subtle fragrance of his cologne announced his presence, followed by a light tap on my shoulder. He stood mere inches away, and the gravity of the moment settled upon me. My palms, covered in sweat, my heart jumping out of my chest. He held two dozen red long-stemmed roses, each of them mirrored the intensity of the last twenty-four hours. His aroma blended with the romantic atmosphere made my knees buckle a little. I could see people slowly shifting their attention in our direction, people stopping and staring, wondering what was unfolding. Every facet of this man was beautiful. He literally took my breath away.

I held the roses, inhaling their fragrance. I closed my eyes, letting my body guide me to a place of calm, a necessary preparation for the conversation ahead. I needed to shut out the world, the noise of the people, the humming escalators, the screeching trains, the jazz musician, the automated announcements, and panhandlers. He took my hand, his touch a gentle lead as he guided me to a quieter, more private area along the platform.

"I've thought about this a lot. I've been wrestling with what to do and how to do it. I know that whatever I do, someone will get hurt. And yeah, I've even thought about just being selfish and looking for something better for myself."

I lowered my eyes. I couldn't look him in the face. "Jamel…" I said, softly.

He gently hushed me, touching my lips with his finger. "Shh, please, just let me speak. I need you to hear me completely before you respond. Did you feel what I felt when we were together?"

"Yes."

"Have you felt anything like it before?"

"No."

"Have you felt like something was missing from your life, but couldn't quite put your finger on it?"

"Yes," I said, wondering how many questions he needed me to answer.

He raised my chin, looking into my eyes. "Do you feel you're forcing things with your husband?"

"Yes," I admitted.

"After our call, my wife asked if I loved you. I froze. She knew something was wrong. She said I wasn't her soulmate, and that she wanted me to be happy, not stay with her out of obligation. I wanted to argue, to beg her to stay, but I couldn't. Deep down, I knew she was right."

"Those are the words I've always longed to hear from my husband, but he never said them. I would've done anything to be the person he needed, just to hear that. And here you are, saying it to me, and I feel like I haven't done anything to deserve it." I struggled to hold back my tears.

He shook his head gently. "Nah, you got it wrong. Years ago, I wrote down this prayer for who I wanted my future wife to be. I kept it forever, but then I kinda gave up and stuck it in an old book. The day we ran into each other, I was going through some boxes and found it. I read it, and it was like, whoa, it was totally about you."

"Jamel, I'm speechless. This is overwhelming." I took a deep, steadying breath, my hand finding its way to my heart as I felt the emotion swell within me.

"Don't say anything yet. Just listen. I want to read to you my prayer."

My legs gave way, and I collapsed onto the bench. Anticipation grew heavy. He unfolded a crumpled paper from his pocket, cleared his throat, and began to read:

"Dear Lord, I ask that you walk with me each day. Forgive me for my sins and how I have treated the women in my past. I am wiser now. I am a man and looking for more. You know the desire of my heart to meet someone special who I can love with my whole heart. Lead me in a way that love stumbles in my way; I can look into her face and know that I have found her. I pray for a woman, beautiful in mind, spirit, and soul. May she be faithful, loyal, sincere, and willing to do whatever it takes to make our love endure forever. Grant her the patience to honor and respect me. Let her be filled with love, humility, and understanding for me and the family we'll create. Give me the wisdom to make and keep her happy and feeling protected. Please cause my path to meet with hers at your appointed time. Amen!" He folded the paper and offered his hand, waiting for mine. He cleared his throat one final time, a tear glistening on his cheek, a clear sign of his deep feeling.

"Does he make you happy?"

He knew the answer, he just needed my confirmation. He could see the despair on my face. Everyone knew our marriage had been over for years.

CHAPTER 12

Week 4
Wednesday Afternoon

I couldn't get out of the parking lot of the school fast enough. Unlike most days, I drove since I had to make multiple stops. Not to mention, my parents were concerned about me being pregnant on public transportation. There were too many scenarios where my high-risk pregnancy condition could turn all bad on the train. Considering traffic, and not having my timing quite accurate, I scheduled the therapy session with enough time for me to get to the hospital, meet with my OBGYN, and return DJ to his mama, all before five P.M. I loved spending time with Derrick Jr. and the opportunity to schedule our appointments on the same day allowed some essential bonus mom and son time. Regardless of the condition of the relationship with his father and me, my relationship with DJ was separate. Our bond was genuine. We built our own connection over time. It took him becoming a teenager to become fond of me, but it happened. I had a way with teens and a gift to gain their trust and affection.

"Bye, Mrs. Covington." I looked over and saw a few students out on the field yelling and waving. I waved back and motioned for them to keep playing and not focus on me.

I sent a text to DJ to be ready outside for me to swing by and grab him and be on our way. Basketball season was approaching, and he needed to get a physical for eligibility.

"What up, B Mama?"

"Hey DJ. Put your bag in the back seat and pop in the front. I'm not your driver today." He chuckled, tossed his bag in the backseat, and plopped in the front. "Did you talk to your dad today?"

"Nope!" He didn't look up from his *Nintendo Switch*. He became engrossed in *Xenoblade Chronicles* before we could even take off.

"You know you can talk to me during this ride." He held his head down, focused on the shooting action.

"DJ... DJ?, do you hear me talking to you?"

"Yeah, yeah, give me one second." He turned the *Switch*, shifting his head in multiple directions. "Ah man! You made me lose!"

"Boy, if you don't put that game console down and talk to me!" I demanded. "How was school?" His face plastered on the screen.

"It was okay." DJ replied reluctantly.

"Okay? Why just okay?"

"I don't know. It just was." He threw his hands up and shrugged.

"When was the last time you talked to your dad?" I asked, knowing that line of questioning would not get us anywhere.

"He texted me last night and asked if I was still going with you to get my physical. I told him I was, and that you would drop me back to my mom."

"Did he tell you anything else?"

"No."

"Well… right now. Your dad and I…"

He immediately cut me off. "It's okay. I know you all are mad at each other right now."

"How do you know that?"

"I'm not a child. I can tell when adults are acting weird. You start wanting to talk to the kids about stuff we don't care about." He returned his attention to his game.

"How do you feel about that?" I asked. I maneuvered into the first available parking space and shut off the engine.

"I don't know." He shrugged again. "You and Dad are always mad at each other. I guess y'all will eventually get over it."

I sat with his response for a moment and thought about how much we unintentionally put DJ through. I even considered all that he already experienced with Derrick and Shayla's relationship. "You know that whatever happens, it doesn't change our relationship, right?"

"Yeah, I know." He picked up his *Switch* and grabbed the form out of his backpack. He lightly closed the door.

We made our way through the parking garage, heading toward the elevator. His appointment was in Family Medicine on the 4th floor and my OBGYN was on the second floor. The plan was to check him into his appointment and get the paperwork signed. I would then come back down to stop by my doctor's office to get clearance for a few additional lab tests my doctor wanted to run.

"DJ, wait one moment." I grabbed him by the shoulder, turning him around to face me. I wanted to look him straight in the eyes. "Your dad and I may not work things out, but the baby will always keep us connected."

"Cool." He said, nonchalantly.

"That's it? That's all you have to say?"

"What do you want me to say? My mama told me this would happen."

I was stunned speechless. I swallowed hard, lifted my chin, and just stared ahead. The elevator doors slid open. The music seemed to echo my bruised emotions. There was simply nothing left to say.

"Hi Ms. Johnson!" DJ darted out of the elevator.

"Hi DJ! Look at you. You're so big now!" Ms. Johnson embraced him, looking him over.

"Ms. Johnson, this is my stepmom."

"Hello. Jamie-Lynn, it's good to see you again. It's been a long time."

"I know. The circumstances were not the best, considering it was a funeral, but it is good to see you as well. You look good!"

"Thank you. How do you know DJ?" she asked in her warm

tone. Her undeniable sweetness radiated from every fiber of her being, enveloping all those around her in a warm and inviting aura.

"Ms. Johnson was my favorite teacher in elementary school," he said with surprising excitement.

"Oh, that's sweet. DJ was one of my favorite students and I'm good friends with his mom Shayla."

"Oh, okay." I did not want to state what was actually on my mind. "How's Lance doing?"

"He's good, still working for TSA. He finally proposed, so we plan to have a wedding next year." Her smile widened.

"You mean to tell me Lance Brown is finally going to settle down? It must be something in the air because I just ran into Charles, and he is thinking about popping the question too!"

"I would say that I was waiting for him to ask, but I needed him to get his act together first. He wanted to do right by me, but it took him a few years to get it all out of his system. We even separated a few years so he could do his thing. We saw other people, but I knew he was my person. Even after the tragic encounter at the diner."

"Wow, I didn't know that." I paused to let that settle in.

She nodded her head. "How are you and Derrick?"

I knew it was coming, and I didn't want her to report anything back to Shayla. It was bad enough she already knew our fate. I searched for a quick response.

"DJ, hurry up and check-in for your appointment."

"Okay. Bye Ms. Johnson." He hurried over to the desk.

I waited until he was out of sight before sharing my lie. "We are great. I'm pregnant." I forced a half smile and pointed at my non-noticeable belly. "That's why I'm here. I have to get a few labs done."

"Congratulations! That's awesome. I know you two have been trying."

The smile disappeared. I didn't want my face to expose my confusion. Shayla knew too much regarding the things happening in our home. "Thank you. Well, I better go. I told Charles to let Lance know we're having a party Saturday night to celebrate Samson's release. You both should come."

"Oh, that's right! Yes, we'll be there. What should we bring?"

"Whatever you bring will be fine. My mama will be happy you're there most of all. It was good seeing you."

I was a little bit nervous while waiting for them to call me in to run the tests. I've been stressed with the entanglement I found myself in, but physically I felt okay. I desperately prayed that the baby was healthy. Considering all the wrong I'd done, I felt I deserved any complications, yet I was still praying for mercy. Preeclampsia was a major fear, especially given my high-risk status due to previous miscarriages and other health problems.

The nurse called me, "Debra Covington." She stood for a moment, glancing around the waiting room. I felt my heart beating fast. I raised my hand and made my way toward the door. The nurse led me over to weigh me and check my blood pressure. My weight was considered normal, only gaining two pounds, but as I sat down, the nurse noticed the distress in my face.

"Mrs. Covington?" she said, softly. "It's going to be okay. Let's take a few deep breaths before I take your blood pressure. I don't want to give a false reading, which will stress you more." Following her advice, I centered myself, Jamel's prayer echoing in my mind. It was a different feeling, knowing I was someone's ideal, someone's prayer, not just a fallback. Calm settled over me as she applied the cuff on my right arm. It tightened, then slowly released—25 over 64. A huge wave of relief flooded me. Everything would indeed be just fine.

The ultrasound showed all was well. The baby development chart confirmed it: my little strawberry was growing about an inch long. I was a mess of emotions, joy mixed with profound sadness. In my fantasies of this moment, Derrick would have been right beside me, experiencing this. But no matter what happened with our marriage, I had made a promise to this child, and I intended to keep it.

Dr. Anson kept the appointment short due to her running behind. She provided me with the official due date and ordered some additional blood tests.

"Remember what I told you Debra," she scolded on her way out of the room. I nodded and folded the paper she handed me. "You should get away for a while and process everything happening in your life. Before you go into the second and third trimester, you will need clarity."

I met DJ in the lobby, and we walked over to the car.

"Is everything okay with my little brother?" DJ asked, unintentionally slamming the passenger door.

I looked over and smiled and started the car. "You mean your sibling?"

"So, you're not going to tell me?"

"Nope." I replied. "Too soon. Give it another two months."

"I don't think I can wait that long," DJ said as he pulled out his *Switch* and continued playing his game.

"Well... you're gonna to have to."

We drove the rest of the way to his house in silence.

When we arrived at Shayla's house, DJ leaned over and gave me a kiss on the cheek.

"Love you," he said before he closed the door.

"Love you too, DJ."

DJ grinned and headed up the steps. Shayla, as usual, gave me a knowing look, quickly replaced by a polite smile when DJ went inside. I waved and drove away. I didn't tell DJ the gender of the baby because I didn't want anyone to know my business just yet. Derrick and I needed to resolve our issues before anything was revealed to Shayla.

CHAPTER 13

Week 4
Wednesday Early Evening

I entered her office. "Before you even ask, he is not coming, and I'm here alone today. I would prefer it that way."

"That's not a problem at all. Sit." Laura motioned toward the couch. "Would you like to tell me what happened?"

"So much I would not even know where to begin." I took a second to think, gather my thoughts, and then sat down. "When I signed up for therapy, it felt like the beginning of the end, but I was like, I gotta try my hardest." My fingers moved almost unconsciously, twisting together and then releasing, a physical manifestation of my internal turmoil. "I needed to prove to myself that I could push past my limitations, that I could grow beyond my comfort zone."

Laura leaned in. "Now that we're alone, I need to talk about what transpired in our last session." She reached out and placed her hand over mine, a gentle pressure to still my nervous fidgeting. "Your well-being is my primary concern." Her voice had changed, taking on an unfamiliar, more official tone. She lifted my chin with a light touch and adjusted her posture to sit more rigidly. "I'm required to ask you some questions that may be upsetting and repetitive, but it's procedure. Are you comfortable proceeding?"

I swallowed hard. "I understand. Ask away." It was clear the hard questions would come. We said too much. This time, I would have to answer them alone and take accountability for my own actions. But this is what I came to do. Face the truth.

"Debra, what are your primary concerns about your own health and wellness?"

"Umm..." Once more, I pulled on each finger. "I am pregnant, so I am trying not to stress." My voice began to quiver. Laura gently placed her hands atop of mine again. She nodded to continue while holding my fingers down. I cleared my throat. "I don't want to lose the baby. There was a time when I was unsure if I wanted to keep it, but I'm sure now. I want to have a healthy baby."

Laura released my hands, shifting back into her perfect posture. "Who currently lives in the home with you?"

"It's just me and Derrick and sometimes his son comes to stay with us, but Derrick has moved out... Well... not officially, but he has been staying in a hotel for now until the smoke clears."

"Smoke clears?" she asked, her eyebrows raised in suspicion, her grip on the pen tightening.

"Derrick and I have been spending time apart. It hasn't been going well."

She nodded, made a notation, and continued her line of questioning. "People often use alcohol, cigarettes, or recreational drugs to reduce stress or feel better. Do you use any of these, including marijuana, cocaine, pain pills, heroin, or methamphetamine? If so, how often? Or how much? Have you ever, in the past?"

"No. Absolutely not! Now, I can't speak for my husband, but for me... no."

"Has your husband ever used any drugs around his son?"

"Not that I know of." Now this could have been interpreted as a lie, but I was not that upset with Derrick for jeopardizing his freedom or the custody of his son. Plus, you can't tell everything. My mama taught me that.

"Okay." She made a check on her notepad. "Do you have any current thoughts to harm yourself?"

"Hurt me? No. If I am honest, I have had thoughts in the past about not keeping the baby." She made another mark on her notepad.

"Have you ever tried to seriously harm or kill anyone else?"

"I've definitely tried to kill Derrick. Duh, don't all wives?" I chuckled, but I saw the look on her face and shifted quickly. "When it gets real intense with me and Derrick, in our heated arguments and tussles, I want to harm him. But nothing too serious. But that was a long time ago. Prior to the pregnancy." It wasn't. I lied again.

"Are you on medication?"

"No."

"Have you ever had services for mental health or substance use?"

"No."

"Have you ever been diagnosed?"

I shook my head. "No."

"Have you ever been hospitalized for medical or psychiatric reasons?"

"No!" My responses were becoming a bit more aggressive.

"Have you had any trauma, like an attack, family disaster, or any type of abuse in your life that has caused you to feel isolated, unsafe, a need for control, distrusting of people or situations?"

"That's why I'm here. Right?"

"Debra, what do you want for yourself?" She dropped her pen and pad and leaned in. "Where do you see yourself in one year that you are not experiencing today or at this moment?"

"Dang, Mrs. Schatz, you know how to get right to it. That's a hard question." I hesitated for a moment to consider if I had even allowed myself to dream in that way. To put myself first and prioritize my mental wellness. I have to admit, I was at a loss. My mind circled and searched for a brilliant answer to give, but I didn't have one.

"Debra, stop thinking, and call me Laura. Close your eyes and take a deep breath." She waited for my compliance. I hesitated, but gave in. I closed my eyes.

She continued, "In and out. Yes, just like that... Again... One last time. Don't give me the answer you want me to hear. Listen to your heart. What are you missing? What do you yearn for? What do you need to be whole at this moment?"

My body shook uncontrollably. Tears rushed down my face and it covered me with chills. I felt a burst of heat surround me like a whirlwind. Laura sat patiently, waiting for me to experience the moment without interruption. Her hands clasped, feet crossed, looking on with concern and compassion.

"I... umm. I want to feel like I'm valued. I feel like I'm constantly shouting, 'look at me, look at me. See me, love me, appreciate me.' I can't catch a break. I know I can't change my past, but I try my best to pour into the lives of my students so they can have a bright future."

Laura stood and approached me. "I want you to hear this: you are enough. You are more than enough. And you will be the most important person in that baby's life." She placed a comforting hand on my back. "What do you truly desire for you and your baby?"

"I want love. I want to give my baby the love I never received. The love I longed for and looked for and tried to manipulate and recreate. And I don't want to do it alone. I want a companion."

"So, you want to repair the marriage with Derrick? I can support you with that."

"Not with Derrick."

"My apologies. Did I miss something? If not with Derrick, then with whom?"

I put my head down. "Well... There is someone else."

"Let me assure you, this is a completely non-judgmental environment. My role isn't to evaluate your choices, offer unsolicited advice, or tell you what to think or feel. I'm here to guide you towards self-awareness, help you reach your objectives, and assist you in making the right choices for your life. Most importantly, I'm here to listen and understand. If additional support is necessary, I can connect you with other professionals. The more you open up, the more I can help."

"I've been seeing someone." I admitted.

"Tell me more." She picked up her pen and leaned in.

"The very first man who took my virginity at fifteen and impregnated me at seventeen years old came back into my life." I stopped short of my next words. Shame and disappointment filled my body.

"It's ok. Please continue."

"It's a recent thing." I tried to justify my indiscretions to prevent her from judging me. "About three weeks ago, I ran into him at the B.A.R.T station, and we exchanged contact information. As you know, things were not going well between Derrick and me. I needed something that was missing in my life. He spoke my language." My heart began to race. I kept my gaze down on the floor. If I was going to get it all out, I couldn't look Laura in the eyes. "I called him that night and after my hair appointment, I met up with him at the restaurant where we buy our fish tacos." The confession leaving my lips brought me right back to the moment.

We were completely captivated by each other, lost in our lively conversation and shared laughter that seemed to never end. Every word he spoke had me hanging on his every syllable, reluctant to part ways. The surrounding air crackled with an electrifying energy. It was as if he had ignited a spark within me, awakening every dormant part of my being in that unforgettable moment. I continued, "I knew that I no longer wanted to be with Derrick. In our five years of marriage, I never desired to be with another man. Even with his cheating and disrespect, I was committed to him. Loyal to *only* him."

Laura listened and jotted down a few notes in her notebook. "Please keep sharing. I am only writing things I want to make sure to return to."

"Since Derrick wasn't talking to me, it was easy. I didn't have to hide anything. We texted all day, every day. He'd say good morning and goodnight. I was incredibly happy."

She was making mental connections, trying to decipher the layers of my narrative. "During our second session, you expressed a desire to remain married and reconcile. I'm curious, was that your genuine self speaking, or was that your alter ego?"

"I wanted to stay married," I said firmly. "It was a last-ditch effort. I needed to know if he felt the same, but he didn't. We both knew it was too late. We came here too late." Her nod showed she understood. We'd believed it was meant to be and tried to force it. The passion had faded, leaving us with nothing but emptiness.

"I'm wondering how you're processing all of this. I have a strong feeling that you're giving up prematurely. This seems to be a recurring pattern of avoidance for you. Your husband came here despite his reluctance, almost as if he needed your reassurance to leave Tatiana." Her response caught me completely off guard.

With a slight tilt of my head, I said, "To be honest, I'm a mix of numb, angry, upset, rejuvenated, and hopeful all at once. But it really seems like you're siding with him!" I straightened my back, crossed my legs with deliberate care, and leaned forward on my elbow, attempting to project an image of composure and control.

She noticed. "I hear you," she assured me. "And please know, I am not taking sides." She set down her notepad and adjusted her posture to mirror mine. "But I need to provide you with a holistic view, Debra. I believe there's something more significant beneath the surface." Yet, as I remained silent, she pressed on, determined to draw out a response from me. "How are you genuinely feeling about the situation with Tatiana? You seem to be avoiding it. You had intense reactions in our second session, followed by a marked disconnection in the third. You're experiencing a tumultuous range of emotions, and we must address them now to engage in meaningful healing."

"I'm so confused. I'm dealing with so much." I strongly sensed she was aiming to manipulate the inner workings of my mind.

She uncrossed her legs and moved forward in her seat. "In our previous session, we covered a lot: your brother being released from prison, actively going through a separation, the turmoil with your parents, your pregnancy, and now the possibility of a new relationship. Do you recognize the pattern here?" She held up her palm, exposing her five extended fingers.

I shook my head. "No, I don't." I was increasingly agitated. "What's the pattern, Mrs. Schatz?"

"Again, please call me Laura." She scooted back in her chair to place some distance between us. "I am sensing an avoidant-dismissive attachment style."

"Now, what does that mean?"

"Essentially, it suggests you avoid intimacy and close connections to protect your independence and avoid being vulnerable. You might find it hard to trust people and tend to hide your emotions in your actions, even while feeling them strongly internally."

"How did you get all that from what I said?" I questioned.

Tilting her head slightly, Mrs. Schatz said, "Debra, I've noticed that when we discuss these significant events in your life, you find it difficult to open up. We saw this with Derrick, and you've shared that it's a pattern within your family. Additionally, your miscarriage at seventeen remains unaddressed. Your wellness is my primary concern. I want you to feel safe and secure here."

"I'm not feeling safe now. I'm feeling exposed. And quite frankly, I'm feeling judged."

"Just to reiterate, this isn't about judgment. My role is to help you become aware of certain patterns, so you can make any adjustments you feel are necessary. I'd like to share a suggestion with you."

"Okay. What's that?"

"I encourage you to grant yourself the time and space to process these significant events in your life. It would be beneficial to hold off on any major decisions until you've dedicated time to your own healing journey."

In my mind, my decision had been made. I was clear about how I felt and what I wanted to do.

Mrs. Schatz went on, "I believe a solitary retreat to process everything would be beneficial. Consider finding a quiet Airbnb outside the city for some personal space, peace, and relaxation. As this is our final complimentary session, I'll provide you with a mindful meditation recording for containment. There are tons of amazing free resources online. I'll start you with the *Loving-Kindness Mindful Meditation* from PositivePsychology.com."

I thanked Mrs. Schatz and exited her office.

"Mrs. Covington! Wait one second."

I almost walked right past her, but something in me said stop and give her a chance. Hear her out. She may have something nice to say.

"Yes?" I aggressively crossed my arms, displaying a sense of annoyance.

"I... I... I want to apologize for my attitude when you first came here."

I perked up and turned towards her, fully focusing on what she had to say, and relaxed my folded arms, ready to engage in the conversation.

She stepped closer. "The only reason I had to stop you today is because you're here alone. I would have said something sooner, but I didn't know how."

"Spit it out! I'm really not in the mood right now," I blurted out, checking my watch for the time.

"Understandable. Your husband slid into my DMs several weeks before I saw y'all come into the office. We exchanged a few messages until I did my own research on him and found out he was married. I found your profile and recognized y'all when you came in."

A wave of frustration washed over me as I shook my head in utter displeasure. "I'm not surprised, but thank you for letting me know." I shuffled around in my purse for my keys.

"I'm sorry for my attitude. I was just really nervous and caught off guard. He completely ignored me when he walked in, and then sent a text telling me not to say anything to you. I can't lie; I felt some type of way." She looked down, clearly regretful.

"Listen, I really appreciate your confession, but it doesn't matter anymore." My fingers located the keys. I continued to search my purse with them clutched in my hand.

"I just want to apologize for my attitude and the negative energy I gave you. You didn't deserve that."

I returned a genuine smile. "Thank you... I really appreciate that." I pivoted towards the exit but stopped abruptly. "Oh wait, I never got your name."

"My name is Darnise Jacobs."

"Darnise? Darnise? Where have I heard that name before?" I spoke under my breath. Suddenly, it hit me like a bolt of lightning. I gave her a thumbs up and waved goodbye, moving closer to the door. As soon as I cleared the building, I couldn't help but chuckle, shaking my head in disbelief.

CHAPTER 14

Week 4
Friday Night/Saturday Morning

It was freezing and dark when Samson walked out of San Quentin dressed in sneakers, a white t-shirt, and jeans. He'd gone in a youth burdened by anger, while we hoped he was returning to us a changed man, I knew the odds were slim. He walked towards the exit, a look of stunned disbelief that he was finally a free man. He took his first free breath in twelve years, a symbolic new start. The cool night air filled his lungs, and he looked up at the moon and stars, feeling grateful for his release. The heavy prison gates resonated as they slammed behind him. Mama, ever intent on control, had meticulously arranged for Michael to be there. She longed to reclaim her "little Samson," yet knew the moment would be too much. After much convincing, she allowed Michael to be the first friendly face. Samson waited patiently as a car approached.

Samson hesitated for a moment. He had no idea who his mother was sending and was under the impression he would have to take an Uber for the first time. The concept of a random person picking him up and taking him to his destination still didn't sit too well with him. He looked around, taking in everything he had missed for over a decade. For years he feared for his safety, developing a thick skin and to prepare for the unexpected. Remaining vigilant at all times, for the moment when anything could erupt on the yard. It was a different world now.

"Yo, Samson!" Michael yelled, snapping him out of his trance.

Samson recognized the familiar face and lit up. "What's up, my boy?" They clasped hands and embraced each other. "You still an ugly nigga!" he stated, laughing and elated to be able to have the moment. He got into the car, feeling an overwhelming sense of relief.

"What's good? It's been a minute, but it's good to see you." Michael continued on rambling in disbelief. "I can tell you've been hittin' dem weights. On some real shit!"

"Aw man, you know I'm just tryin' to get like you, dawg." He offered back. Seeing Michael's fresh set of wheels caught his attention. "This you?" Samson asked, smoothing over the dashboard and inspecting the interior.

Michael simply smiled and nodded. He looked Samson over, shaking his head in disbelief that he was free. Offering water and snacks, he hoped to ease any hunger. Michael wanted to make him feel like royalty, a welcome home fit for a king. He was finally going back to his family, leaving that stark prison cell behind for good.

"I know yo' ass is hungry. What do you wanna eat? It's on me!"

Samson smiled. "Take me to the nearest spot that has food. I have been dreaming about some chicken wings."

The neon sign flickered above the door. The diner was a cozy place, and the smell of fried chicken filled the night air.

The streets were empty, and the only sound was the click-clack of his shoes on the pavement. A sense of loneliness gnawed at his heart, and he wondered if he would ever be able to rebuild his life again. He had seen things that would haunt him for the rest of his life. But he had also learned some valuable lessons. He decided not to dwell on the past and instead focus on building a better life for himself.

"You good?" Michael questioned, noticing that Samson was a bit uncomfortable.

A brief hesitation flickered across his face, a moment of uncertainty about entering. Yet, the insistent rumble in his stomach overruled any doubts, and his legs carried him through the door. It had been an eternity since he'd known the satisfaction of a proper meal. The diner was vacant except for an older gentleman behind the counter, who raised his eyes from his newspaper and asked, "What can I get ya, son?" The question was clearly directed at Samson.

They found seats at the worn counter, and the old man filled two mugs with steaming coffee. He addressed Samson directly, "Son, I might not know much about the law, but I know this: every day is a new chance to make things right."

Samson looked up at the old man. "My guy, what are you talking about?"

The man pointed to the paper bag of belongings seated next to him on the adjacent bar stool. Samson looked down and gave him the nod to show understanding. Samson was so used to watching over his belongings, he didn't even notice he could have left them in the car.

"We seem to be the first stop for many bruthas just wanting a good hot meal. No judgment at all. I just understand and it's good to see you out!" He placed a freshly cleaned glass down next to the coffee and poured him a glass of ice water and slid the menu in front of him. Michael put up his hand, signaling to the old man that he was not hungry and to take care of Samson.

A nod of relief passed over Samson, as if shedding a heavy burden. He sipped his coffee and looked out the window and saw the first rays of dawn breaking over the horizon. He knew he had a new day, a new life, and a new beginning. Gratitude filled him. He was also deeply thankful for the hot plate of food in front of him. The haunting memories of prison food, quickly being replaced by the comforting aroma of fried chicken and mashed potatoes. But as he ate, his mind wandered to the years lost behind bars and the paths he could have taken.

"I'm just glad to see you lookin' good. You don't have to say nothin'. Enjoy yo' food. I got you." Michael patted his brother on his back and kept a watchful eye on the door and his ride through the window.

After finishing his meal, they stepped out of the diner and got back into the car. It was time to go home, but first he had to meet up with one of the shorties he had been writing while locked up. She gave him her address and told him where to find the key when he was released.

"Aye yo,' Mike, I need you to drop me off by Bushrod Park in North Oakland."

"Say less. I already know."

CHAPTER 15

Week 4

Saturday Night

"Everyone be quiet. He's about to come through the door." Charlene warned, trying not to ruin her well-thought-out-surprise.

The door slowly crept open.

"Surprise!," we all belted out, uncoordinated. Had we taken the time to practice, we may have been more in sync.

"Mama, you didn't have to do all this," Samson responded, grinning from ear-to-ear. "Aye!" He noticed and recognized some of the faces standing before him. "But I'm glad you did." He hung his head and clasped his hands together, taking in the moment. It looked like he may have whispered a quick prayer. Samson lifted his head and poked his chest out.

"Welcome home, Son." Daddy walked over and embraced him with a half-hug, half-handshake. They held their embrace for a moment and released. "No matter what, you're still my son." He kissed him on his cheek and gave him another pat on his back.

Samson was beaming with joy as he hugged everyone and

thanked them for coming. Mama ran over to the speaker and turned up the volume, doing her little two-step. She knew E-40 was one of Samson's favorite rappers. She set down her glass of wine and ran over to her son and held him tightly.

"My baby's home. My baby's home! Thank you, Lord!" She turned to the party. "Y'all don't know how much I prayed and cried that my baby would make it back home safely. Thank you, God!" She was now on the verge of tears. Mama released her grip on Samson and hit her little two-step again. Grabbing his hand and twirling him around, she embraced him one last time.

When she looked up, we made eye contact, and she gestured for me to join them. Intense nervousness washed over me, along with a deep uncertainty. I ran through countless versions of what might happen. I imagined an emotional reunion, tears and embraces, or his usual teasing, of him hitting me upside my head–playful but slightly aggressive. Or, worst case, he'd figure out I had something to do with his arrest and try to take me out right there in the middle of the living room. All these scenarios swirled in my mind. I was completely unprepared; I shifted my focus and acted as if I hadn't noticed her.

"Debra Tucker, get yo' ass over here and greet your brother," Mama yelled to me, signaling for me to come over.

"Yeah, Sis." Samson cosigned, "don't act like you ain't happy to see me!"

I couldn't initially tell from his tone where he stood yet.

The sound of the doorbell distracted the moment, and Mama

hurried over to let in the waiting guest. I motioned in Samson's direction.

"Now we can get this bitch started!" Derrick raised up his case of beer and casually pushed past my mama to see who was in the house.

"Excuse me Derrick, you betta show me some love coming up in my house! I'm actually surprised to see you." Charlene looked over in my direction, hoping her rhetorical statement would be addressed.

"My bad, Mama." He kissed her on her cheek and squeezed her tightly. I could tell he had already pre-gamed before coming. He was loud and leaning to the side. There's no way this night would end well. "Somebody tried to leave me off the guest list." He shot his eyes at me. All I could feel were daggers.

The pressure suddenly intensified, becoming almost unbearable. The challenge was twofold: confronting my brother and, simultaneously, maintaining a convincing role of a happy with Derrick to conceal our troubles from the gathered family and guests. I froze, overcome with anxiety. I desperately wished I could just blink out of existence.

"Debra, get yo' ass over here and show me some love!" Samson demanded. "Plus, you need to introduce me to yo' man. I wish I could say I heard a lot about the nigga, but you never responded to my letters." He gazed back at me with a condescending look, as if I were insignificantly small in comparison.

Gradually, I felt the return of sensation to my limbs, and I approached Samson to confront my deepest fears. He pulled me close, holding me tightly. I surrendered to his embrace, and the tears began to pour, unstoppable. We stood there, suspended in time, weeping in each other's arms. We were completely alone. A rush of childhood memories flashed before me, and a wave of guilt and regret crashed down. *What had I done?*

"Baby, step back, let me meet the man of the hour." Derrick tugged back on my shoulder to peel us apart. "We're not doing all that crying shit. This is a celebration. My man is home from the pen. He is ready to get fucked up!" he slurred out.

"Samson..." There was no introduction needed. "This is my husband, Derrick."

Derrick slapped his hand, grabbing it and went in for the hug. "Pleasure." Derrick placed his hand on his chest and bowed his head. "Debra has told me a lot about you."

"Baby, do you want me to make you a plate?" I quickly interrupted, because I did not want Derrick to start speaking recklessly.

"Of course, I want some food. I'm hungry as hell. I need something to soak up some of this liquor I've been drinking."

I grabbed him by his hand and escorted him away to the kitchen.

"What are you doing here?" I made a deliberate effort to keep my voice to a low volume. "We haven't spoken for days; you haven't been at the house. Why are you poppin' up all of a sudden?"

"I wanted to see you. I can't come and be wit' my wife?" He moved in closer. His hand was poised to touch my face, but I saw his motion and sidestepped the caress.

"Whoa, hold on! You can't just—all of a sudden I'm your wife again?" I exclaimed, backing away and frantically looking around. "You're out of line, and you came to stir up some mess." I leaned in, my voice a tense whisper. "This ain't the time nor the place for it." My eyes darted around, scanning the room. My head was on a constant swivel, desperate to ensure no one was within earshot and that my parents were nowhere to be seen. "You have to leave now. Please! We can talk when we get home."

"Hell nah, I'm staying. You can't tell me what to do. I'm a man!" He was beginning to make a scene. I know Derrick and if I engaged with him, he would go there. All I needed to do was to convince him it was his idea to go. Stroke his ego a little bit.

"Baby Girl, come on back in here so we can make a toast to Samson," my daddy commanded from the next room.

"Okay, Daddy." I yelled back. "Let's go back into the living room, do the toast, and we can go home together." I picked up his hand and placed it on my face. "I've been missing you."

"Oh, you have? How much have you been missing me?" I placed my finger on his lips to stop him from speaking and leaned in for a long, passionate kiss. I gently caressed his back and let him wrap his hands around me.

"That much!"

He backed away slightly, his eyes burning into mine, sucking his teeth. He was ready to take me right there. I won't deny it; I felt the pull too. It had been weeks since we'd touched. I'd almost forgotten the feeling. I craved more. I kissed him again, my temperature rising. My hands moved to his back, exploring. He tightened his grip, his kiss becoming more insistent. He touched every part of me in that kitchen. I was so lost in the moment, I wouldn't have cared if the whole world was watching.

"Oh Baby, you wasn't lying." He came up to breathe for a moment.

"I guess not." I surprised myself. "Let's go, make our rounds, so we can get out of here."

"I like that." He smacked my booty as we left the kitchen and entered the living room.

Daddy raised up a glass and asked everyone to quiet down so he could share some words with the guests.

Ding Dong.

"Dammit! I'm gonna make my toast. Why the hell can't Black people be on time to a surprise party?"

The interruptions were now like clockwork. Mama ran over to the door and greeted her best friend Linda, fashionably late as always, with her highly anticipated fried chicken, baked macaroni and cheese, and okra medley. Following behind, was Charles, his guests, Lance, and Jamie-Lynn, with a tray of freshly baked cookies. They must have met outside and waited to enter together. Mama's planning did not disappoint. She had managed to gather everyone together to celebrate and encourage my brother.

"Does everyone have a glass? Somebody get my baby a glass of champagne." She paused for a moment to catch her breath and take it all in. Our older cousin darted into the kitchen to grab the special goblet for Samson.

Ding Dong.

"Okay, now we ain't never gonna get this toast done if we keep stopping to open the door," Daddy complained. "Just unlock the shit and let the late folk let themselves in."

"Okay, baby, I'll leave it unlocked."

"Hey girl!"

"Oh no! I should have left it locked." Charlene joked. "I'm playing girl, hurry up and get in here. You made it just in time for the toast."

"Hey everybody, I brought wine and champagne, and it looks like I'm right on time!" Raquel sashayed into the house, overtaking the spotlight in the only way she knew how. "Heeeyyy everybody!" She slipped past Edmond and gave him a wink. My dad returned a smile and motioned for her to hurry-up and get somewhere so he could complete the toast.

Given their strange and tangled history, it was remarkable they were even being civil. Undeniably odd, but they had, with some effort, come to a mutual agreement to tolerate one another. It was then that Edmond observed Raquel's unawareness of Charles, and he made a swift decision. He paused the planned toast, gently placed his glass on the table, and with a subtle gesture, invited everyone to get back to their conversations.

"Oh, who is that handsome young man?" Raquel pulled down her shades just low enough to peek her eyes above the brim.

"That's my husband, so back up!" I teased. Knowing she had some almighty kryptonite WAP to bring any man into her web of destruction.

"Okay, you better keep him close, Debra. Damn, he is fine!" She pushed her shades up, found a corner to post up in, but then her attention was instantly caught by someone across the room. Raquel immediately abandoned her spot and practically ran over to him.

"Charles! I can't believe it's really you," she exclaimed, her eyes filling with tears of joy.

He nodded, his own eyes displaying more emotion than he had anticipated.

"It's good to see you, too, Mama," he replied, ensuring his voice remained firm and composed.

Raquel's eyes locked onto Kayla, and she smiled back warmly. "And who's this little angel?"

"This is Kayla, my daughter," Charles proudly declared, as he placed a comforting hand on her shoulder. "Kayla, this is your grandma." Raquel's heart swelled with joy as she slowly absorbed the significance of the moment. Despite only hearing whispers about Kayla and the lack of communication with Charles, this very moment marked the first time she was able to witness the beauty of her granddaughter up close.

"Grandma? Absolutely not," she said with a playful shake of her head. "It's Glamma, honey. I'm far too fabulous and youthful to be a Grandma."

Kayla shyly waved at Raquel, not quite sure what to say.

"Mama, I've been wanting to talk to you about something," he began, taking a deep breath. "I know it's been a long time since we've spoken," he hesitated. "Can you please confirm if Calvin's my biological father?"

Raquel's expression darkened as she glanced down at her hands, regret evident in her eyes. "Charles, I deeply apologize for not being honest with you earlier. Are you absolutely certain you want to talk about this now, especially in front of Kayla?"

He nodded, affirmatively and motioned for her to proceed. "I don't keep anything from her."

"Listen, I need you to understand the situation wasn't black and white. I made some regrettable choices in the past, but it was all for your protection." She glanced over at Kayla. "I got pregnant with you when I was young, wild, and dumb. I didn't want to tell anyone, so I just let everyone assume that Edmond was your father. Him included. I messed up, I know. But I didn't find out Calvin was your real dad until much later."

Charles was overcome with a pang of sadness and anger. "Seriously, my entire life was a lie? Come on, Mama," he said firmly. "You should have told me."

"I'm really sorry, Charles," Raquel said, tears rolling down her face. "I hope you can forgive me at some point. I'm not asking for anything from you today, but you're my little baby and I just can't handle this anymore."

"Mama, I'm grown, not a baby! This time taught me I need

to be responsible and figure things out myself. I always relied on you to fix my problems, runnin' to you to get me out of shit. I had to mature these past years, and they've actually been good for me. I'll always love you, but it'll take time to fully trust you again. Let's take it slow. Let's focus on building a relationship with Kayla and see how things go from there." Charles embraced Kayla and gently pressed a sweet kiss to the top of her head.

"I can work with that." Raquel leaned in for a hug and Charles accepted it. They just stood there for a few moments; the weight of the revelation heavy in the air.

"Ahem!" Edmond cleared his throat and tapped on his glass with a spoon, feeling like it was now the best time to proceed.

Derrick came up behind me, placed his hand around my waist, and held me tight.

Daddy glanced over at me, smiling, and started his speech. "Now that we're all here and settled, I have a few words I would like to say," he said, puffing out his chest. "As the man of this house, I have accepted the responsibility of keeping everyone in my home safe. I haven't always been great at that; sometimes, my ego has gotten in the way." She drew nearer to him, a gentle hum escaping her lips, clearly showing her agreement. "What I'm trying to say is, Samson Tucker, I love you. I'm proud of you, and I can't wait to see what you do with this second chance at life. To my boy!" Everyone raised their glasses and took a sip of their champagne.

"Okay. Now's our chance…" I whispered to Derrick, pushing him away from the crowd.

"Debra, I know you're not trying to sneak out of here without speaking to me. And who is this handsome fellow?"

"Hey, Miss Lydia." I responded, following her orders. "Derrick, this is my mama's best friend, Miss Lydia." Derrick took her hand and gently kissed it.

"I know that's right. You betta' watch him, Debra." Lydia blushed, keeping her eyes glued on Derrick. "I know his type."

"Believe me, I know his type too!" I joked.

"It's been so long since I've seen you. Let me see that belly; you know yo' mama told me you were pregnant."

"Shh!"

"What? Is it a secret?"

"We don't want everyone to know until we are clear!"

"Now you know Miss Lydia doesn't know how to whisper and I'm too damn old to be keeping secrets. That baby's going to be fine."

"We're just not making any announcements right now. This day is all about Samson."

"Alright, alright, I understand. But let me know if you need anything. That's my little niece or nephew you're talking about, after all. And since Lance ain't havin' no babies, I'll have to live through you."

"Mama, I can hear you." Lance hissed from the adjacent room. "And congrats, Debra."

"See, I told you I can't whisper."

"Well, it was nice meeting you, Miss Lydia, but I gotta get my wife home." Derrick winked, so she understood the urgency of the situation.

We quickly turned around and headed back to the kitchen, sneaking out the back door so we didn't have to bump into anyone else. I could already hear my mama fussin' at me for not sticking around to help clean up or say goodbye, but we just had to seize the opportunity.

"Mama, I just saw Debra slip out the back door with Derrick. Is everything okay?" Samson asked.

"What? You mean to tell me that little heifer left without helping me clean up? And she left with Derrick?" she shook her head in disappointment. "He probably told her she had to go. I don't think he likes her being around her family."

"Do I need to go handle that?" Samson requested, eager to get back into protective mode.

"No, baby. This is your party. We can deal with them tomorrow."

"Hey, Mrs. Tucker, do you need any help with anything before me and Kayla head out? We just wanted to stop by and show some love."

"That's sweet, Charles. I think we have everything covered."

"Samson, come holla at me real quick before I get out of here." Charles motioned for Samson to join him for a private conversation.

"No doubt."

"How are you feeling?" Charles asked.

"Bruh, I'm just grateful to be out. A nigga was cooped up and caged up for a minute, and I'm glad to be free."

"I hear that. But how are you really doing? You good? You need anything? I can shoot you some bread. We brothers and I got you."

"Bruh, I appreciate that. Right now, I am solid. San Quen' had solid programs, and I studied a lot. I really worked on myself. I dedicated a lot of time to personal growth and rehabilitation. I was a wild boy when I went in. I participated in some anger management groups and shit, even earned my Associate's degree up in the bitch."

"Word? That's what's up. Well, you look good. Look like you was hittin' dem weights too."

"You know I still gotta look good." Samson poked out his chest with his chin up in the air. They both laughed and clasped hands.

Charles brought Samson in close. "How much you know about that nigga, Derrick?"

Samson answered, "What Debra don't know is that I've been keeping tabs on her inside. I knew about that nigga before she married his ass. His people used to run with the Neighborhood Kings."

"That's where I recognize his ass from. I knew he looked familiar, but I couldn't put my finger on it. Now, you know I didn't fuck wit' Calvin like that, but that gorilla is still in our blood."

"Say less, I'm already on it. I know he been puttin' his hands on her too! She thinks I don't know that shit. I acted like I didn't know who he was when he came in tonight."

Charles looked over at his daughter, who was watching both of them talk. "Kayla, go over and say your goodbyes to your grandma," he yelled over to her to get her out of earshot. He turned back to Samson. "Her mama is Tanisha Watkins." He paused so his words could sink in.

Samson's eyes widened as he ran his hands over his face. "Fuck! That means that was her uncle?"

Charles nodded his head. "Exactly. I have to keep a close eye out on her, and you, because I know the streets are talkin'."

"Damn. I did not think this shit would come full circle like this."

"You need to lay-low for a few weeks while I figure some things out. I need to put a few things in place to make sure nothing happens to you."

Samson crossed his arms and leaned towards Charles. "Say less. I'll post up here until I know it's good."

"Good. Let me know if you need anything."

"I appreciate you, bro, for real. You're one of the ones who came and got up wit' me while I was in. That's love."

"I told you I got you. You're my li'l bro, and I gotta look out for you."

"Charles, you out already?" Lance inquired, slapping his hand and bringing him in for a hug.

"Yeah, man. I gotta get Kayla back to Tanisha. I don't want her blowing up my phone." He checked his phone, his expression suggesting a mutual understanding of the situation.

"See, that's what yo' ass get fo' tryin' to put that baby on me! Karma's a bitch." They both laughed.

"But I'm glad it happened, because Kayla is my world."

"No doubt. It's good to see you. We don't get up like we used to." Lance switched his attention from Charles to greet Samson. "It's good to see you, too. You look good. I see they took care of you in there." Lance went in for the bro hug and patted him on his back.

"You know. Yo' boy is somebody." Samson joked, stroking his chin, grinning from ear to ear.

"He held it down on the inside, while I kept it straight on the outside. Ain't no kin to Calvin gon' be anything less." Charles added.

"True!" Lance nodded. They all understood. "I saw you talking to Mama Rocky. Y'all good?"

"We're good for now. I want Kayla to have a relationship with her. So how I feel doesn't matter right now. Even though I didn't have a relationship with that man. He left everything to me. I got to keep it all together for Kayla."

"I feel that," Lance replied. "Let me get out of here and get back to my lady."

Charles smiled. "It's good to see y'all still together."

"You didn't believe me when I told you she was the one. She made a nigga lay down his playa life. I love that girl! She means the world to me, and I want to keep her happy."

"That's what's up. We'll connect later. Just hit me up." Lance left them in the kitchen.

"Remember what I said Samson, lay-low for a while. Hit me if you need anything."

CHAPTER 16

Week 5
Sunday Morning

"Debra, open up! I know you're in there!" Samson pounded furiously on the front door. "Little Sis, open up the door." Samson relentlessly hammered on the door. "Dammit! Open the door! Please. I just want to talk to you."

I could hear him from our bedroom. I knew this moment would come and I could no longer run from it. He was here now. I rolled over and placed the cover over my head, hoping he would just go away.

"Why is your brother here?" Derrick sat up, wiping the sleep out of his eyes. "Why is he knocking on our door like that? Tell him he gotta go before I do," he warned.

He was back at home. We had a wild, passionate night that left me more confused than I needed to be. He apologized and made love to me over and over, as if he needed me to believe his words through every stroke. "Baby, it's fine. I need to talk to him. I can't avoid him any longer."

"I don't know if I like that. You told me he's dangerous, and that's why you had him locked up." Derrick reiterated; his tone filled with slight concern in his voice.

"Debra, I know you're in there." Samson yelled, now peeking through the window.

"I know what I told you, but he's still my brother. He would never hurt me, and I have to face him. I'm tired of lying to him."

"A'ight. I'm right here if you need me." I kissed him gently and reached for my cover up and sweats to be half-way decent to meet with him on the porch.

"Debra, I'll bust this window if you don't come and open the door!"

"I'm coming! Damn. Samson, you don't have to do so much. It's early in the morning. What do you expect?" I removed the deadbolt and cracked open the door.

"I expect for you to talk to me when I come home from being locked up for twelve years. I expect you to spend time with yo' family instead of running off wit' some mothafucka who puts his hands on you. You thought I didn't know?"

"Samson, keep your voice down." I quickly opened the door and rushed out before he got too loud. I closed the door behind me.

"Oh, so you don't want him to hear me? Are you choosing him over yo' blood? I don't give a damn if you're pregnant."

"Samson, it's too early for this shit. Calm down."

"Calm down? What the fuck, Debra? What's gotten into yo' stupid ass? I got eyes and ears everywhere. I know he put his hands on you, runnin' around these streets wit' different bitches, and you're going to defend him?"

"Sam…" Derrick pulled open the door, strong-arming me to the side to confront Samson.

"I think it must be me you're looking for."

Without hesitation, Samson's balled fist slammed into Derrick's left cheek. Derrick, clearly shocked, instinctively cradled his face. He swung a clumsy punch in return, but missed his mark. Samson delivered another forceful blow, forcing Derrick crashing to his knees. I quickly moved to Derrick's side, desperate to shield him from Samson.

"Samson, stop!" I shouted.

Samson ignored my requests and forcefully punted Derrick in the stomach with his fresh Jordans.

"Don't you ever put your hands on my li'l sister."

Derrick raised his right arm in surrender, a gesture of defeat. He dabbed at the blood trickling from his mouth and then pressed a hand to his side, catching his breath. After a moment, he struggled to his feet and retreated into the house, grumbling, "This shit's on you!" It was a shock to see Derrick finally defend me, but at the same time, he'd absolutely brought this on himself.

I plopped down on the steps and buried my face in my lap. "I'm sorry, Samson."

"You don't have to apologize to me. I've been gone, and it was my job to protect you." He wiped the sweat from his forehead, panting a little.

"No. You don't understand. I'm so sorry. It's all my fault! I ruined your life. I told the police you killed Tony." I blurted out, with no hesitation.

Samson chuckled and shook his head. He turned to me. "This is not your fault. You don't get how any of this works. The cops don't care if somebody snitches. There is a bigger plan in the works."

I perked up and lifted my face from my lap, confused why this amused him. "I don't get it. What are you saying? You aren't mad at me?"

"*I* agreed to be a Neighborhood King and there was no way I could get out and I didn't want *out*, *I wanted in*. I needed to be a part of something. This had nothing to do with you. I did what I did."

"I don't get it. I thought my confession the day they arrested you at the funeral got you locked up."

"That's because you watch too much TV."

"I killed Calvin for Mama. We both knew what would happen next."

Shock and terror overtook my face. "What??"

"The first time I rode with Calvin Rogers, he claimed to be my father. I didn't believe him until I asked Mama. When she was upset with Dad, and staying with Big Mama, she confessed everything but told me to keep it a secret. When Dad called Raquel and left her out-of-the-loop again, she had it. Calvin constantly threatened her, saying he'd tell Dad about their affair and that I wasn't his biological son, and that he'd take everything from her."

"What??" I replied, still in shock, not anymore convinced that he was telling the truth.

"I knew I had to kill his ass. I was prepared to go to prison, well, at least jail, and Mama would get me out."

Charlene was always steps ahead. Why didn't I know about any of this? All the secrets and lies.

"Mama kept all of this from Daddy? How could she do this? How could you?"

"She said she'd tell Dad when it felt right. I was already angry with him and didn't care. He treated Mama like shit and forced her hand. I knew we were different and always clashed. It was almost like he knew all along and wanted me to pay for her mistake."

"Samson, slow down. You're not making any sense. What was the bigger picture? The day of the funeral, you were arrested for killing Calvin Rogers, but they convicted you of killing Tony Watkins because of what I told the police when we went to the police station."

"That's where you're wrong, Sis. Check this out… Calvin had me kill Tony Watkins because he tried to kill Charles that night at The Shadow Bar but ended up killing Elijah instead. Calvin had me kill Tony because he went after his son. Regardless of how they got down, that was still his blood. Street code. What none of us knew was that Elijah was an informant. The cops had been trying to get to Calvin for years. I bought the gun from Elijah. They already knew. I was supposed to get life, but since I killed him, they cut my sentence down."

"Oh, my God."

"They already knew I was his son, and they knew about Charles. Charles works with the Oakland Police Department."

"So, did Elijah set you up?"

"Of course he did! He was saving his own ass!"

A wave of relief washed over me. For years, I'd carried the guilt of being responsible for my brother's incarceration. Hearing that freed me. "I can't tell you how relieved I am."

"You're still fucked up. We're not going to skip past the fact that you wanted me locked up. After everything I've done for you, looking out for you. You would still try to put me behind bars. You're sick!"

"Me? You all made me this way! Nobody cared about me. I was always in your shadow."

"You're delusional, Li'l Sis. You were Dad's pride and joy, you were his 'baby girl.' *I* was never good enough. I did everything wrong, so you had an easy shot. You're the only one who's truly a Tucker. While you're crying about simple shit, I always felt disconnected, like I didn't belong. I knew my answer was in the streets and I found it. Stood face-to-face with it and destroyed it before it would destroy me."

"I'm sorry. I never knew how you felt."

"Of course you didn't. Everybody has always protected you from the truth and reality. You got to live in fantasyland. You had nothing to worry about."

"You don't know that!" I spat back, trying to defend my trauma.

"You got this man up in your house that puts his hands on you, and you like it! He runs around the streets with other bitches, and you tolerate the shit. There is a part of you that always runs toward drama. And you don't have to. I went in one way, but I've changed a lot, but it seems to me like you're still the same."

I didn't want to admit he was right. My pride wouldn't let me. I didn't need him to tell me about me. Hell, Mrs. Schatz had already done that in so many ways. That's why I went to see her in the first place. Here I am trying to teach students about the consequences of making mistakes while making huge ones of my own. I've been running from myself for years, pointing the finger at everyone else because it felt good. I've been lost and alone and deep down, I hoped the baby would provide me the comfort and connection I've been longing for.

CHAPTER 17

Week 6

Thursday Evening

I inhaled deeply, packing my essentials for my grand exit. Contrary to my expectations, leaving wasn't the liberating experience I'd pictured. I'd hoped anger would shield me and I'd embrace freedom with joy. Instead, I demolished three mini packs of donuts, emptied two boxes of tissues, and sobbed every five minutes.

My temporary stay at an Airbnb was set, paid for, while the San Leandro lease was still pending. The thought of remaining in our home was unbearable, knowing the constant stress it would cause. Derrick's resistance to my leaving only made things harder. Even considering legal options felt futile, as I was certain he'd make things as difficult as possible. So, I chose a different path, leaving him with what he needed to finally move forward. Our sessions with Mrs. Schatz had revealed the toxic, abusive nature of our relationship, and that we were both to blame. This decision was for my own health and for the sake of my unborn child. And as Samson said, I needed to get myself together and find my own answers.

"So, you're really leaving me?"

"Derrick, I told you. After everything with Samson and my family, I can't repeat the cycle. Too much damage is done." I defended myself, piling all my bags by the front door.

"So, what we shared meant nothing to you?" he asked, hoping to get some emotion out of me.

"It did, but... it is too much. I can't trust that you will keep your word. I'll leave the key under the mat. Once I'm settled, I'll let you know where I'll be, and we can figure out the co-parenting plan."

"So that's it? It's like that?"

"That's it. It's like that. I'll always love you, but I can't do this anymore." I hung up quickly, before I lost my resolve. I mentally marked him as done, took a deep breath, and dialed the next call with a heavy heart.

"Hello?"

"Hey Tatiana, I have to tell you something. This may come as a surprise to you, but I'm leaving my husband." I announced, with no formal introductions or hesitation. Ripping the band-aid was more comfortable in order to not prolong the inevitable.

"Oh, my goodness, Debra. Are you okay? What happened? That was not a part of the plan," she requested frantically, confused.

"I know. I know. It's just been a long time coming. I've tried to keep up with the charade, but I can't do it anymore."

"I don't understand. This was your plan. Am I supposed to stay with him now? I'm ready to move on too," she said, sounding confused rather than upset.

"Break up with him, too!" My hands grew sweaty. I shifted the phone to my other hand to keep a good grip. "But I also have some other news... I'm pregnant."

"Pregnant?" Tatiana questioned, surprised that there was more to this confession. "That's amazing news! Congratulations, Debra. I'm happy for you," she paused for a moment to ensure she was not jumping the gun. "Are you happy about this?"

"Uh, I don't know yet. I guess so, but I'm still kinda skeptical."

"I totally understand. With all that you've been through in the past, I know you don't want to get your hopes up. Oh, the irony."

"I know, right? I guess God doesn't like the games I'm playing. How about you? Have you heard from the doctor yet?" I inquired.

Tatiana hesitated a moment before answering, "Debra, I'm sorry. I haven't told anyone yet, but... I had a miscarriage a few days ago."

"How? Are you okay? We have been monitoring everything, and you were good. The baby was fine."

"Derrick doesn't know yet." Her pause lingered, prompting me to remain silent, allowing her to express all that weighed on her mind. "Does this mean I need to give you back the money?"

"Girl, I don't care about that money. Are *you* okay?"

"I think I'll be. This plan was getting out-of-hand, anyway.

It's probably best this happened, considering you're pregnant now. You would've had two babies!" she chuckled.

"This is true. I *am* pregnant and things are looking good. To me, it was money well spent. It's over with Derrick, and I'm moving on with my life."

It was liberating to unleash all the secrets and embark on a guilt-free life. I would never admit to Derrick that I hired Tatiana as a gestational surrogate, and that I paid her to start a relationship with him. The thrill of testing his true intentions was undeniable. Initially, I wanted to see if he would go for the bait. I had suspected it would be all too simple, given his reputation as a womanizer who lacked self-control. He just couldn't keep his dick in his pants. Aware of the potential risks of another miscarriage, choosing a surrogate was a strategic decision to ensure a successful pregnancy and the arrival of a healthy baby. *My* pregnancy was an accident. It was never a part of the plan. I was careless. After I confirmed Tatiana was pregnant, the plan was to leave Derrick and have my baby.

I met Tatiana one afternoon during my lunch break. I promised Kelman I would support his family's business, and I did. I was immediately struck by her grace and skill as she rolled cigars, and I couldn't shake the thought that she was exactly the kind of woman Derrick would be drawn to. I'll confess, perhaps I'd watched one too many Lifetime movies, leading me to consider some rather unconventional possibilities. I made several return visits to the cafe before I befriended her. She was cool, and if I were into girls, I would've totally asked her out. But I wasn't that curious. She told me about her money problems and wanting to go back to school. Plus, she was into polyamory, which was interesting to me. Against the backdrop of my own increasingly strained relationship with Derrick, I began to see an unusual opportunity with Tatiana. Despite some initial hesitation, her openness and genuine interest in my proposal made her the perfect candidate. I presented her with a generous offer of $20,000 to serve as my surrogate, a decision that felt surprisingly right for both of us. I showed her a picture of Derrick, and her immediate attraction to him further solidified my plan. We proceeded to create a formal contract, which we both signed, and I transferred the first installment of the agreed-upon sum a few weeks later.

Choosing surrogacy was a deeply challenging decision. The inability to conceive naturally left me feeling overwhelmed and powerless. While Tatiana appeared to be a strong candidate, we knew medical and psychological evaluations were necessary. Thankfully, before things got really bad, we took the significant step of registering with an agency and freezing embryos, waiting for the right match. Getting Tatiana registered with our selected agency was the final piece. It was important to me that our baby still had genetic ties to the both of us.

"Yeah, I know things didn't go exactly as planned, but hey, I'm glad you got what you wanted," Tatiana said, breaking the stillness.

"Look, it's up to you what you do with Derrick, whether you break up or not, that's your thing. But I'm done. We're going to figure out this co-parenting thing."

"I'll call him today and see if we can meet. I'll tell him about the miscarriage and the breakup, but you need to tell him the rest."

"That's fair. So, I guess I'm breaking up with you, too. I'll have my attorney handle the paperwork for the miscarriage and contract termination. Take care of yourself."

"You, too!"

CHAPTER 18

Week 7
Sunday Morning

D^{ong... Dong... Dong...}

Before beginning the practice, please find a comfortable posture that will help keep your spine straight, either seated or lying down, wherever is comfortable.

Next, pay careful attention to the positioning of your hands. When sitting, rest them in your lap or place them gently, palms down, on your knees. When lying down, keep them by your side.

Now, breathe naturally as we shall begin the meditation.

I drew in a long breath, held it for a moment, and then slowly released it.

Visualize a loved one sitting directly in front of you, united by a radiant white light that flows between your hearts. Allow yourself to deeply immerse in the emotions of love and tenderness that you hold for them.

Enjoy the feelings as they fill your body.

Next, slowly focus on the phrase, 'May I be well, happy, and peaceful,' feeling the warmth of loving-kindness filling your body...

And send these feelings to your loved one. 'May you be well, happy, and peaceful...'

Breathing naturally... As the light connects you, heart to heart.

'May I be well, happy and peaceful...'

'May you be well, happy, and peaceful...'

Feel yourselves bathed in the warmth and light of loving-kindness... while repeating these phrases silently...

"May you be well, happy, and peaceful..." I whispered.

Remember to breathe naturally, as the white light connects you both, heart to heart, and continue 'May you be well, happy, and peaceful...'

I whispered again, "May I be well, happy, and peaceful..."

As you continue to breathe naturally, visualize the white light surrounding you transforming into a powerful circle of light enveloping both of you. Feel the energy and protection this circle of light provides, creating a strong and positive force field around you both.

Bask in the comforting embrace of the light, enveloping you in the soothing energy of love and compassion that emanates from within you and radiates out to envelop your surroundings...

Embracing every living creature, from the tiniest insect to the mightiest beast... reaching beyond our planet to encompass the vastness of the universe.

Imagine you and your loved one exuding a radiant glow of boundless love and kindness that extends endlessly into the universe.

"May we be well, happy, and peaceful. May all beings be well, happy, and peaceful…" I chanted.

Breathing naturally, repeat these phrases silently. 'May we be well, happy, and peaceful… May all beings be well, happy, and peaceful…'

Now, experience the delightful sensation of warmth and a powerful sense of expansion coursing through your body. Embrace the profound connection with your heart as it radiates positive energy out into the universe. Feel the genuine friendliness that emanates from within you, creating a harmonious bond with the world around you.

"May we be well, happy, and peaceful. May all beings be well, happy, and peaceful…" I repeated.

Immerse yourself in the soothing embrace of loving-kindness. Focus on your body and tune in to the sensations and emotions coursing through you. Take a moment to acknowledge the observer within you, the serene presence that neutrally witnesses all, free from any bias or criticism. This awareness is a tranquil and unchanging part of your being, always there to guide you through life's ups and downs.

Breathe naturally…

And slowly open your eyes.

The wind chimes hung from the back deck of the small cottage. The mountains painted an amazingly rich, picturesque backdrop, with birds chirping, as they dipped into the water well. Off in the distance, you could hear the faint sounds of dogs barking.

The clouds powdered the blue sky above. I was surrounded by cactus and clusters of fragrant white sage decorated with silver-white leaves, and white flowers with lavender streaks. Peace was an understatement.

I noticed the bunnies hopping across the dirt gravel that led to the unpaved roads, the Mountain Bluebird hovering a few feet above the ground. I checked my phone. Still no bars. The faulty reception allowed me to unplug, even when I wanted to check in with the chaos. It was so peaceful. Sounds of dripping water from the stone water well had never brought me so much joy. When Mrs. Schatz recommended getting away from it all, I initially wrote her off. I was a Black woman in the middle of nowhere watching the field squirrels scurry about. I watched the red-tailed hawks, American Kestrels, and Loggerhead Shrikes with their hooked bills and black masks soar over the fences and in and out of the isolated bushes. The excitement of a deer off in the distance brought me back to childhood. Why was this my first-time experiencing nature like this? I felt deprived, then rejuvenated.

I broke from my trance as soon as I heard the car pulling into the driveway. The Airbnb was secluded, except for the hosts that stayed on the property in their camper. I wasn't sure if he would find the place since it was situated off the main road. I slipped on my cozy slippers, grabbed my glass of non-alcoholic sparkling rosé, and opened the door.

Book Club Discussion Questions

Chapter 1 Discussion Questions

1. Debra and Derrick's therapy session takes an unexpected turn when the therapist reveals information Derrick disclosed on the paperwork. How does this impact your understanding of their relationship and communication dynamics?

2. The therapist, Laura Schatz, uses a specific approach to therapy. What are your thoughts on her methods? Do you think they are effective?

3. Debra expresses her frustration with the receptionist's attitude. Have you ever encountered a similar situation where you felt judged or dismissed? How did you handle it?

4. Derrick reveals a significant part of his past involving his first love, Shayla, and their son, Derrick Jr. How does this revelation affect your perception of him?

5. Debra reflects on her parents' relationship and the impact it has had on her own views on love and marriage. How do generational cycles of dysfunction manifest in the story?

Chapter 2 Discussion Questions

1. Debra's encounter with Jamel, her childhood crush, brings up a significant event from her past. How does this unexpected reunion complicate her emotional state?

2. The conversation between Raquel and Lanette touches on themes of family secrets and societal expectations. What are your thoughts on their perspectives?

3. Debra's internal conflict about her marriage and pregnancy intensifies. What factors contribute to her indecision?

4. The setting of Oakland plays a significant role in the story. How does the city's diversity and complexities mirror the characters' experiences?

5. The chapter ends with Raquel revealing a long-held secret about her childhood. How does this revelation shift the dynamics of the story?

Chapter 3 Discussion Questions

1. Debra's visit to her parents' house reveals the family's anticipation of Samson's release from prison. How does each family member react to the news?

2. The conversation between Debra and her parents highlights differing perspectives on family, responsibility, and forgiveness. Which perspective do you relate to most?

3. Debra's announcement of her pregnancy leads to a discussion about the timing and circumstances of having a child. What are your thoughts on the various viewpoints presented?

4. The chapter delves deeper into the complexities of Debra's relationship with Derrick. Do you think their marriage is salvageable?

5. The chapter ends with a poignant conversation between

Debra and her father. How does his advice impact her understanding of her situation?

Chapter 4 Discussion Questions

1. Debra's interaction with her student, Redd, sheds light on the challenges faced by young people in the community. How does Debra's role as a counselor and mentor contribute to the story?

2. The chapter explores the physical and emotional effects of Debra's pregnancy. How does this impact her daily life and interactions?

3. The chapter ends with a confession from Kelman, leaving Debra in a state of embarrassment. What are your predictions for the next chapter?

Chapter 5 Discussion Questions

1. Debra and Derrick have a tense exchange during their therapy session. How does this conversation reveal the state of their relationship? What are the underlying issues and unspoken resentments that surface during this confrontation? How does Derrick's reaction to Debra's questions affect your perception of his character?

2. Debra shares her fears about her pregnancy and her ability to be a good mother. Why does she feel so insecure about this? Who does she confide in, and what kind of support does she receive? How does her vulnerability in this chapter make her more relatable or sympathetic to the reader?

3. Secrets and hidden information continue to play a significant

role in this chapter. What secrets are being kept, and why? How do these secrets impact the characters and their relationships? How does the author use the theme of secrets to build tension and suspense in the narrative?

4. Despite the challenges she's facing, Debra expresses a desire for things to get better. What is she hoping for? What steps, if any, is she taking to achieve these changes? How does her hopefulness contrast with the difficulties she's experiencing? What do you think the future holds for Debra and her relationships?

Chapter 6 Discussion Questions

1. Debra has a strong sense of déjà vu and a feeling that this pregnancy is different from her past experiences. What do you think contributes to Debra's feeling that this pregnancy is a turning point? How does her internal dialogue about breaking "the cycle of dysfunction" and finding "joy and serenity" reveal her state of mind?

2. Derrick arrives at the doctor's appointment late and disrupts the flow of the conversation. His behavior is often dismissive and controlling. How does Dr. Anson handle Derrick's presence? How does Debra react to his behavior? What does Derrick's behavior reveal about his character and his relationship with Debra?

3. Dr. Anson asks if Debra and Derrick want to know the baby's gender, and Derrick immediately assumes it's a boy and makes a dismissive comment about having "two girls on the way." Debra, on the other hand, emphasizes wanting

a healthy baby above all else. What do these contrasting reactions reveal about Debra and Derrick's priorities and expectations for the pregnancy? How does this interaction highlight potential conflicts between them?

4. Dr. Anson slips Debra a note when Derrick isn't looking, what do you think is on the note? Why does Dr. Anson feel the need to speak to Debra privately? What does this suggest about the doctor's concerns for Debra's safety and well-being?

Chapter 7 Discussion Questions

1. Tanya shares a detailed account of Derrick's conversation at the barbershop, revealing his frustrations with Debra and his relationship. How do you feel about Tanya sharing this information with Debra? Is she being a good friend, or is she stirring up trouble? How might this information impact Debra's perception of her marriage and her next steps?

2. Derrick's comments at the barbershop reveal his dissatisfaction with his marriage, including his feelings about Debra's appearance, their lack of intimacy, and his preference for Tatiana. What do these revelations tell us about Derrick's character and his communication style? How do his words contrast with his actions towards Debra in previous chapters?

3. Debra reveals to Tanya that Jamel was her "first" and that she had a miscarriage in college that Jamel never knew about. How does this revelation change your understanding of Debra's past and her connection to Jamel? Why do you think she kept this information from Jamel? How might this past experience influence her current feelings and decisions?

4. At the end of the chapter, Tanya senses a shift in Debra's tone when she reveals her pregnancy and asks, "Oh no! Is everything okay? I know I just went in and didn't even check-in with you." What do you think Tanya is picking up on? Why do you think Debra is hesitant or unsure about her pregnancy despite wanting it? How does this contrast with Derrick's behavior and the information revealed at the barbershop?

Chapter 8 Discussion Questions

1. Debra describes feeling utterly depleted and unwilling to play Derrick's games, stating that the only reason she attended the session was because it was free. How does this reveal Debra's current emotional state and her perspective on the marriage? What does it say about the value she places on the counseling sessions, and how might this impact the effectiveness of the therapy?

2. The chapter highlights a significant disconnect between Debra and Derrick, both in their personal interactions and their approach to therapy. They arrive separately, avoid each other, and have drastically different reactions to Laura's questions. How do these interactions reflect the overall state of their relationship? What are the key communication breakdowns you observe, and how might these be addressed?

3. Debra admits to lying about wanting to keep the baby to agitate Derrick, and she also reveals her "alter ego," a protective presence she can "switch on and off." What do these revelations tell us about Debra's coping mechanisms and her internal struggles? How do these actions relate to

her feelings of numbness and fear, and what might be the long-term consequences of these behaviors?

4. Laura offers Debra resources for a support group and chatline, emphasizing the importance of connecting with other women, especially expectant mothers who have experienced trauma. Why do you think Laura makes this suggestion? How might Debra benefit from this type of support, and what challenges might she face in accepting or utilizing these resources?

Chapter 9 Discussion Questions

1. Charlene and Edmond have a long history and a complex relationship. How would you describe their dynamic at the beginning of this chapter? What are the main sources of tension between them?

2. Edmond expresses regret about not accepting Samson fully. Why do you think he struggled with this? How does the revelation of Samson's true parentage affect Edmond's feelings?

3. Charlene says, "I'm sure God used Samson to straighten us out." What do you think she means by this? Do you agree with her perspective?

4. The conversation between Charlene and Edmond reveals past infidelities and hurts. How do they navigate these difficult topics? Do they handle them well?

5. Edmond says, "Debra's all I got." What does this statement reveal about his feelings and priorities? How does it contrast with Charlene's focus on Samson?

Chapter 10 Discussion Questions

1. Debra describes a strong sense of déjà vu during her encounter at the hotel. She says, "It wasn't him I was making love to, not really. It was the man who had always had my heart…" Who do you think this "man who had always had her heart" represents? Is it a past version of the same person, an idealized version, or someone entirely different in her mind?

2. Debra acknowledges that "the present held the greater weight" despite the pull of the past. She also recognizes the encounter as "a risk, potentially a setback, but I felt no regret." What do you think motivates Debra's decision to proceed, despite knowing the potential consequences? Is she acting impulsively, or is there a deeper reason behind her choice? Do you agree with her assessment that it was "worth the risk"?

3. The passage is filled with vivid imagery and sensory details, such as "the stillness of sitting in bed and staring at nothingness," "the soft glow of the lamp," and "his eyes devoured every inch of my body." How does this descriptive language contribute to the overall mood and atmosphere of the scene? What emotions do these details evoke in you as a reader?

4. Debra describes her heart and soul as being "laid bare before him" and feels that she is "exactly where I was meant to be, in the arms of the man who remained my truest love." Do you think Debra's feelings are genuine in this moment, or is she romanticizing the situation? Is she finding solace in the present, or is she potentially setting herself up for

more heartbreak? What clues from the text support your interpretation?

Chapter 11 Discussion Questions

1. At the beginning of the chapter, Debra is avoiding Jamel's call but is also secretly hoping he will initiate contact. Why do you think she is experiencing this conflict? What does it reveal about her emotional state and her marriage?

2. "He was the platter, and I was starving for attention." Debra describes her feelings towards Jamel in this way. What does this metaphor suggest about her emotional needs and her relationship with Derrick?

3. Both Debra and Jamel are married. Discuss the ethical implications of their interactions and the choices they are making. How does the chapter portray the complexities of infidelity?

4. Debra reveals to Jamel that she was pregnant when she left for college. Why do you think she chooses to share this information now? What is the significance of this revelation?

5. Jamel reads Debra a prayer he wrote years ago. What is the significance of this prayer? How does it impact Debra's feelings and the direction of their conversation?

6. Can you relate to any of Debra's or Jamel's feelings or struggles in this chapter? Why or why not?

Chapter 12 Discussion Questions

1. Debra has a unique relationship with Derrick Jr. (DJ),

Derrick's son. How would you describe their bond? What does the way Debra interacts with DJ reveal about her character, especially in the context of her strained relationship with Derrick? How does DJ's nonchalant attitude towards his parents' issues affect your perception of the family dynamics?

2. In this chapter, Debra lies to Ms. Johnson about her relationship with Derrick, claiming they are "great". Why do you think Debra chooses to lie? What does this reveal about her internal conflict and her desire to maintain a certain image? How does this compare to her honesty (or lack thereof) in other areas of her life, as seen in previous chapters?

3. Debra experiences a range of emotions in this chapter, from anxiety about her pregnancy and health tests to sadness about her relationship with Derrick. How does the author portray Debra's emotional state? What specific moments or details highlight her inner turmoil? How does her emotional state influence her interactions with others, particularly DJ and Ms. Johnson?

4. Debra is navigating her high-risk pregnancy while also dealing with marital issues and family drama. How does her pregnancy contribute to her sense of isolation or vulnerability in this chapter? How does the ultrasound scene, where she imagines Derrick by her side, emphasize this feeling? What does Dr. Anson's advice about "getting away" and processing everything suggest about Debra's needs at this time?

5. DJ makes several insightful comments about his parents' relationship, showing he is more aware than they might

think. How does DJ's perspective contribute to the reader's understanding of the situation? What does his statement, "My mama told me this would happen," reveal about the dynamics between his parents and his own feelings about the situation? How does his focus on his video game serve as a coping mechanism, and what does it say about how children process adult conflicts?

Chapter 13 Discussion Questions

1. Laura asks a series of direct and probing questions about Debra's health, safety, and mental state. Discuss the purpose of these questions. How do they make Debra feel? Do you think Laura's approach is effective? Why or why not? How does this questioning reveal potential underlying issues Debra may be experiencing?

2. Debra admits to seeing Jamel and describes their interactions. Why does she choose to reveal this information to Laura? What is she hoping to achieve by sharing this secret? How does her confession about Jamel relate to her feelings about Derrick and her marriage?

3. Laura suggests Debra has an "avoidant-dismissive attachment style." What does this mean? Do you agree with Laura's assessment? What evidence from the chapter supports or contradicts this interpretation? How does this attachment style impact Debra's relationships and decisions?

4. Laura advises Debra to give herself some time to process everything she is going through and suggests taking a trip alone. Why does Laura give this advice? Do you think it is

good advice? What are the potential benefits and drawbacks of Debra following this suggestion? How does this advice reflect Laura's understanding of Debra's situation?

Chapter 14 Discussion Questions

1. The text describes Samson experiencing "a look of stunned disbelief" at his freedom but also feeling "a sense of loneliness" and remembering things that "would haunt him for the rest of his life." How do you reconcile these contrasting emotions? What do you think is the biggest internal struggle Samson faces in these initial moments of freedom?

2. Michael is portrayed as a supportive and welcoming figure. How does his presence and actions (offering food, a ride, etc.) impact Samson's transition from prison to the outside world? What role does Michael play in helping Samson feel like "royalty" and like he is "going home"?

3. The diner scene is rich with symbolism. What is the significance of the old man's words, "every day is a new chance to make things right"? How does the diner setting itself contribute to Samson's sense of a "new day, a new life, and a new beginning"?

4. The text mentions Samson thinking about "all the time he had lost in prison and how he could have used it differently." How does the author balance the weight of Samson's past with his hopes for the future? Do you think Samson will be able to truly leave his past behind? Why or why not?

Chapter 15 Discussion Questions

1. How does the family react to Samson's return? What are the

different emotions and dynamics at play during his "welcome home" party? How does Charlene try to manage the situation? How does Edmond's reaction compare to Charlene's?

2. Describe Debra's initial feelings and reactions to seeing Samson again. How does their interaction play out? What is significant about their emotional embrace? How does Derrick's interruption affect the dynamic between Debra and Samson?

3. Derrick is clearly intoxicated and disruptive. How does his behavior impact the party and the family dynamics? Why do you think he acts this way? How does Debra attempt to manage him? What does this reveal about their relationship?

4. The toast keeps getting interrupted. What does this series of interruptions symbolize? How does it contribute to the overall tension and atmosphere of the party? How does each new arrival change the mood or dynamic?

5. Raquel's arrival brings a new layer of complexity. How does her interaction with Charles and Kayla unfold? What is the significance of her revelation about Charles's paternity? How does this revelation change your understanding of the family history and dynamics?

6. If Michael had been present at Samson's homecoming celebration, how would his interactions with other characters and Samson himself have altered the party's atmosphere? What could be the author's motivation for choosing to leave Michael out of this key scene?

Chapter 16 Discussion Questions

1. Samson arrives at Debra's home and is immediately confrontational with her and Derrick. What drives Samson's anger and behavior? Do you think his feelings are justified, considering his past and his relationship with Debra? How does his return after 12 years in prison influence his perspective and actions?

2. Debra is caught between her brother and her husband. How does she feel about Samson's presence and his accusations against Derrick? What is she trying to balance or protect in this situation? How does her revelation to Derrick about Samson's past impact her decisions at that moment?

3. Derrick steps in to confront Samson, leading to a physical altercation. How do you interpret Derrick's actions? Is he defending Debra, or is there something else driving his response? How does the fight change the dynamics between Debra, Derrick, and Samson?

4. Debra reveals to Samson that she was the one who told the police about him killing Tony. Why does she confess this now? What does she hope to achieve by telling him the truth? How does Samson's reaction surprise or confirm your expectations?

5. Samson provides a detailed account of the events leading to his imprisonment, revealing a complex web of relationships, secrets, and motivations. How does this new information change your understanding of Samson's character and his choices? What are your thoughts on the motivations of Calvin,

Charlene, and others involved? How does this revelation affect Debra and her perception of her family?

Chapter 17 Discussion Questions

1. Debra orchestrates a complex and somewhat manipulative plan involving Tatiana as a surrogate and a test for Derrick's fidelity. What do you think about Debra's motivations and methods? Was she justified in her actions given her past experiences and suspicions? How does the revelation of her own pregnancy change your perspective on her choices? Discuss the ethical implications of her actions, considering both her own well-being and the impact on others involved.

2. Despite planning her "grand exit" and hoping for freedom, Debra experiences a mix of sadness, guilt, and anxiety. Why do you think she struggles so much with leaving, even though she believes it's the right decision? How does her conversation with Tatiana, including Tatiana's miscarriage, further complicate Debra's feelings? Discuss how the author portrays the complexities of leaving a relationship, even a toxic one.

Chapter 18 Discussion Questions

1. Debra finds solace and clarity in nature. How does the author use descriptions of nature to reflect Debra's inner journey? What symbolism or metaphors are present in the natural elements she observes? How does her connection with nature contribute to her healing process?

2. Debra is expecting a visitor at the Airbnb. Who do you think

it is, and why? What are Debra's hopes and fears about this potential visitor? How does the anticipation of their arrival contribute to the suspense and tension in the chapter? What does this anticipation reveal about Debra's desires and needs at this moment?

Acknowledgement

I really appreciate everyone who kept asking when the sequel would be out! Honestly, those questions kept me going when I felt stuck. Your questions were a driving force, helping me overcome challenges and find the story's path. The time away to experience life, including love, heartbreak, and loss, has deeply influenced this book.

A special acknowledgment goes to my husband, Cameron E. Parr, and my sister, Tabia Norris, for their crucial role as beta readers. Their collaborative feedback shaped the storyline and ensured a better reader experience. I also deeply appreciate the unwavering support of my family and friends, who contributed to even selecting the cover design. This publication is a testament to teamwork, and I want to thank everyone who played a part: Nicole Walker, Lucy Giller, and Samia Asif.

For those of you who have been on this ride with me since 2016, thank you from the bottom of my heart. "Beyond the Hurt" was the start of it all, and it's what led to Revision Publishing LLC, where I get to help other authors bring their dreams to life. We're just getting warmed up! I'd be so grateful if you'd leave a review online and let me know what you think. Your feedback might even make its way into the next book. What are you curious about? Who are your favorite characters? Whose story should I dive into next?

Connect with me on social media @AkilahTrinay or via my website: www.revisionpub.com.

About the Author

Sharifa "Akilah Trinay" Parr is building her legacy. She is not waiting for someone to open the door of opportunity for her—she is creating it. Growing up in Oakland, CA, Akilah Trinay could see dreams deferred and visions manifested and ultimately had a choice to make.

As a self-publisher and consultant, she has a passion for helping people bring their ideas to life and share them with the world. With a background in education, communications, public relations, and a strong understanding of the self-publishing landscape, she has helped many clients successfully publish and promote over 25 titles in various genres, languages, and formats.

In addition to her publishing expertise, Akilah also has a wealth of knowledge in various fields, including business, marketing, and personal development. She uses this knowledge to provide valuable consulting services to clients, helping them to refine their ideas and strategies, and achieve their goals. Akilah received a B.A. in Communications with an emphasis in Public Relations from California State University, Los Angeles and an M.A. in Educational Teaching from Alliant International University. She is currently pursuing her doctorate in Educational Leadership at Saint Mary's College of California. Apart from her successful role as CEO of Revision Publishing LLC, she is also an educational specialist and co-founder of Our Collective Impact LLC, a published author, podcast host, entrepreneur, wife, and mother.

Also by Akilah Trinay

- Beyond the Hurt (Book1)
- Potty-Training Day: For Boys
- Día de entrenamiento para ir al baño: Para niños
- Potty-Training Day: For Girls
- Día de entrenamiento para ir al baño: Para niñas
- Potty-Training Day Coloring and Activity Book: For Boys and Girls
- Self-Publishing Made Simple Workbook: A Comprehensive Guide to Successfully Self-Publish Your Book

Beyond the Hurt

As with the streets of Oakland, California; three families' lives intersect and are bound by blood ties, secrets and deceit. Each one, desperate to put their sordid pasts behind them, has strived to create the perfect life for themselves and their children. Consumed with the petty criminal activities of their children, as well as dealing with their own trust issues with each other, each parent will do anything and everything to protect their legacy. However, when the actions of three friends attract the attention of an Oakland kingpin, hidden truths and long-buried rivalries bubble to the surface. A case of mistaken identity that ends in murder shakes the very core of each person involved. Are they able to come to terms with their past transgressions and move ahead to a clean future, or will the secrets and lies lead them down a path of destruction? The streets of Oakland are waiting and watching.

Available on Amazon or www.revisionpub.com

Made in the USA
Columbia, SC
18 June 2025